The Border Bunch

The Border Bunch was rampaging around Santa Rita, robbing stages and bullion consignments and running off cattle. Santa Rita needed a marshal, a tough lawman to take the place of the one ambushed and shot from his saddle by Border Bunch riders.

So the town got Jeff Barradell, a gunhawk with a none-too-honest reputation. They said he was a killer, that he turned a partner of the owl-hoot trails over to the law in order to gain a pardon for himself. How could this leopard change his spots?

Barradell pinned the law-star on his vest and pushed his gun into the bullet-slashed set-up around that small border town in southern Arizona – and men wondered where his sympathies lay and what would happen to them. They didn't have to wait long to find out!

The Border Bunch

ANDREW GREY

A Black Horse Western

ROBERT HALE · LONDON

ISBN 0 7090 6934 0

Robert Hale Limited
Clerkenwell House
Clerkenwell Green
London EC1R 0HT

Typeset by
Derek Doyle & Associates, Liverpool.
Printed and bound in Great Britain by
Antony Rowe Limited, Wiltshire

ONE

Winter came whispering down out of the Whetstone and Dragoon mountains with a chilly breath that year and with it came Jeff Barradell, riding under a name that was not his own.

Barradell rode a big bay gelding with the air of a man who was lonesome and liked being so. He was lean and looked almost as mean as a winter-starved coyote; he wore the garb of a wanderer of that region: dusty jeans and scuffed boots, a red flannel shirt and buckskin vest, a bandanna about his neck and sun-warped sombrero on his head. About his middle was a bullet-studded holster belt; the holster hung low on his right leg and there was that in Barradell's make-up that told a man he could grab the Colt .45 it housed out of its leather pretty quick.

No one asked Barradell where he came from, where he was going or what his business was; they didn't ask any man questions like that in Arizona Territory in the early eighties.

Barradell went up the mesa to Tombstone at almost

midday, housed his horse at a livery stable, ate in an Allen Street restaurant then angled his long-legged way across to the Crystal Palace where he ordered a beer.

A small man, scrubby bearded and in the dusty garb of a miner, stood close to him with a schooner of beer gripped in a horny fist. He was of the talkative kind and said to Barradell, almost without looking at him:

'The Border Bunch has been hell-raisin' again. Raided the railroad depot over at Mescalero Wells day before yesterday, I'm told. Got away with a payroll that was comin' in for the Satisfaction Mine.'

'That so?' answered Barradell with no marked interest.

'Yep. They're a mighty hard-boiled bunch, that crew.'

'They are for sure.' There was still scarcely any notable interest in Barradell's tone. He drained his schooner, shoved it across the bar to the barman and indicated a refill by clinking the price of another drink beside the foam-flecked vessel.

'Banks, payrolls, cows, stages an' trains – ain't nothin' that Border Bunch won't steal if they get within' smellin' distance of it,' commented the old miner philosophically. 'Nothin' a-tall.'

'Seems that way,' the lean newcomer answered, taking a grip on the handle of the newly-filled schooner. For the first time since he opened the conversation, the small man glanced at Barradell squarely and the Colt in the low-slung holster leaped to his eye at once. He lifted his eyes cautiously from the gun-gear around the lean man's middle and concentrated on the thin, lantern-jawed, but not unhandsome features under the dusty halo of the black sombrero brim.

In the midst of the scrubby beard and straggling moustache, the old miner's mouth became a tightly drawn line. He watched the lean stranger partake of his beer with a quiet relish. In his mind, a little voice said: *'By grab! Me an' my big mouth – he looks mean enough to be one of the Border Bunch – I never saw him around this town before!'*

Jeff Barradell continued to drink in his leisurely fashion, quite aware of the suspicious gaze of the oldster. He finished his beer and placed the schooner down on the bar, nodded a terse farewell to the old miner and strode out of the Crystal Palace with a click of spurs.

Out on the street, a sharp chill pervaded the clear desert sunshine which touched warped false-fronts and dusty adobe structures with a golden patina. Winter was coming on, for sure.

Horses and burros, hitched at intervals along either side of the street, shifted around resentfully and turned their rumps to the keen wind that whipped small flurries of dust out of the wheel-tracked and hoof-punctured ground. Barradell cuffed down the brim of his hat and made for the livery stable where he had left his mount. He stepped into the roadway, catching sight with a corner of his eye a large, range-garbed individual standing on the opposite side of the street. Barradell moved for the livery stable as if he had not noticed the tall and broad man across the street. Nevertheless, the features of that individual were extremely familiar to him and he knew the big man was watching him with a keen interest.

He moved unconcernedly through the door of the tall livery establishment and turned his head slightly as he paid for his gelding's feed. He could see the wide sweep of one section of Allen Street, but the large man had disappeared.

Barradell mounted up and took the gelding out of the stable, turning its nose for the south. After a minute of riding, he turned his head slowly and saw the big man, mounted on a dun-coloured bronc, turning out of the Allen Street end of the OK Corral and riding at his back.

'So that's why he disappeared,' Barradell mused. 'Went to get his cayuse, an' now he's followin' me.' He pulled his lips into a hard smile and directed an unspoken remark towards the big man following him: 'You ain't developed any more brains than you had back in Texas, Bull!'

Barradell rode easily, allowing the rested and newly-fed mount to take its own pace. He did not turn his head once, but knew the big man on the bronc was following the whole time.

Out of Tombstone, he took a narrow desert trail that snaked clear of the flats and twisted through a tumbled and up-ended terrain of dunes and rock-clusters.

'I'll give you a break, Bull,' he mused. 'I'll take you

into the rough country an' save you the embarrassment of ridin' after me on the flats, where you could be seen for miles.'

He paced the horse through the tangled land where yucca and saguaro grew in profusion, then halted it abruptly as he rounded a high-rearing rockpile. He came out of the saddle swiftly, yanking his six-gun clear of leather as he did so, hitched his rein around an arm of saguaro cactus and squatted on his heels, Mexican fashion, behind the rockpile beside the trail. Gripping the Colt, he waited with a tight grin on his lean features.

The tramp of hooves on gritty shale came and grew louder. The big man who had followed him out of Tombstone rounded the rockpile at a steady walk. Jed Barradell said:

'Yank yore rein an' lift yore paws!'

The big man's jaw dropped open and he almost fell out of the saddle as he found himself looking straight into the uptilted snout of the Colt in the hand of the man who squatted beside the trail with a grin that held no humour. His pudgy hands grabbed back his rein and the bronc reared back to a halt.

The big man had heavy and stupid features, bronzed by south-western sun and bristled with a three-day blue beard. He lifted his hands quickly. Fear of the grinning man was evident in his eyes.

'Don't shoot, Barradell!' he wheezed.

'You're a lousy tracker, mister,' commented Barradell. 'I knew you were there ever since you turned yore cayuse out of the OK back in town.'

'Don't shoot, Barradell,' quavered the big man again. 'I didn't mean no harm, honest!'

The hard grin lingered on Jeff Barradell's face.

'What're you callin' me that name for, mister?' he asked. 'You don't know me, my name's Slim Smith!'

The big man held his hands high in the air and a frown of bewilderment puckered his brow.

'Smith? Yore Jeff Barradell, the gunslinger that was once marshal of Comanche Peak in Texas—'

'An' a lot of other places,' added the squatting, grinning man, 'but you ain't goin' to shout about it, Bull. See? My memory's as good as yore's, I remember you – Bull Claffin, small-time cow-thief out of the Big Bend country. You never did stack up to much, Bull, except as an idiot. What're you doin' in this territory an' why were you foilowin' me?'

'No reason, honest! I saw you back in Tombstone an' thought it was you – I just wanted to find out—'

'So you tailed me out on to the desert,' grunted Barradell. 'You must think I'm as big a fool as you. Are you in with this Border Bunch, Bull?'

Bull Claffin wriggled in his saddle.

'No, I don't know nothin' about 'em, honest!'

'What're you doin' in Arizona? Texas is yore stampin' ground.'

'Driftin', just driftin'. I'm goin' straight an' honest since the Pony Creek crew was broken up – I'm lookin' for work!'

Barradell knew the mounted man was lying. Bull Claffin had once been a minor member of a Texas rustling crew which Barradell had helped to break up, so minor and so much the dupe of cleverer men, in fact, that he'd been allowed to walk free out of court while the others were given penitentiary sentences. His presence here in Arizona, close to the region where the murdering, plundering Border Bunch was active, needed some explaining.

'Lookin' for work, eh, Bull?' Barradell said. 'An' you followed me just to satisfy yore curiosity. If I thought you were mixed up in anything around here, I'd ventilate you here an' now. Fact is, I have a notion to do it right now!' He made a slight motion with his six-gun and the big man jumped visibly.

'No! Don't shoot! I'm not mixed up in anythin' an' that's the truth!'

'Who's runnin' that Border Bunch, Bull – who's the brain of the outfit, d'you know that?'

Claffin, with his hands in the air, was wide-eyed and chalk-faced.

'I don't know anythin' about the outfit, I tell you!' he declared. 'I'm not mixed up with 'em, I'm driftin' – looking for a wranglin' job!'

Jeff Barradell came up slowly from his crouch and holstered his Colt. Bull Claffin brought his hands down with obvious relief.

'I think you're a liar, Bull, an' I know you're a fool, but I'll give you some advice: get back to yore driftin' an' find yoreself a job, but make sure it's with some cow-outfit north of Tombstone – don't come south of the town or I'll plug you as soon as I see you!'

Claffin gulped.

'You wouldn't do that, Barradell, not you—'

'The name's Smith', cut in Barradell, 'an' what makes you think I wouldn't?' He narrowed his eyes and contemplated the big man with a bleak stare. 'Remember what they say I was before I turned marshal?' he asked.

Bull Claffin licked his heavy lips and started to form the answer in hesitant words.

'Yeah, they say you – you were—'

'A gunslick – a professional killer an' an outlaw who sold out his partner for a free pardon, like a lot of lawmen have done in the past,' Barradell finished icily. 'That was a long time ago, Bull. I don't see any reason why I should tell you whether it's true or not, but when I say I'll kill you on sight, I mean it. Keep north of Tombstone an' if there are any more of yore kind around, tell them to do the same. Turn yore cayuse an' vamoose!'

Bull Claffin required no second bidding. He yanked his rein, turning the bronc about and paced it quickly around the rockpile in the direction of Tombstone.

Barradell took a few steps into the middle of the trail and watched the heavy mounted figure ride around another outcrop of yucca-fringed rock. Maybe Claffin was telling the truth, he thought, but his excuse for having tailed him out of town was lame in the extreme. Still, the big man was a lot more of a fool than a knave and he could be discounted as a force to be reckoned with.

Barradell unhitched his gelding, swung into leather and resumed his south-bound journey. The sun was sliding down from its noon zenith now, colouring the spiny land with orange rays and the approach of the moderate south-western winter had gentled its intensity. Barradell rode, thinking of his encounter with Claffin – it was an echo of that bullet-slashed rustler round-up back in Texas when he'd been marshal of Comanche Peak. Maybe Claffin had spoken the truth and maybe not; may be he was treading the path of honesty, looking for a place in a ranch bunkhouse for the winter – and maybe he wasn't.

A purple mistiness began to sift down over the rugged sweeps of the high Huachucas and Barradell touched spurs to the flanks of his gelding, urging it along the trail at a faster pace.

Night would fall soon in these short end-of-the-year days and a rider, lost in the desert's element of timelessness, would find it upon him almost before he realized it.

Barradell wanted to reach his destination after sun-down but, even so, not too late.

Santa Rita was the lean rider's destination.

It nestled under a mesa in the wide, sun-punished and wind-eroded land where Arizona merged with Mexico. Santa Rita was in Arizona, but it was Mexican by name, Mexican by design and the culture of Mexico was dominant within it.

Barradell came to the town when night lay thick on the desert rims and the high mesa. He took his gelding slowly along a single, rutted street that opened on to the usual plaza, became a straggling street again then died in the desert. He had seen many such towns:

adobe buildings, sun-crumbled, standing alongside occasional wooden ones; a twin-towered Spanish church; a well in the centre of the plaza; more Mexicans than Americans; horses, burros, flies, smells and lonesome, haunting drift of guitar music.

Barradell paced his weary mount along the street which was lighted only by the yellow lamplight blooming from windows on either side of it. He rode with his head slightly bowed, so the shadows of his wide hat-brim was cast on his face; his eyes assimilated the scene as he progressed. On one side of the street. he saw a squat adobe building with a single, barred window. Painted on the wall over the door, in irregular characters, was the legend: 'Town Marshal' and, in smaller lettering, barely discernible in the poor light: 'A.J. Poindexter'.

Almost directly across the street, was a wooden store, fronted by a gallery. A board running the length of the sun-warped awning was inscribed: 'Timothy Mannix, General Store'. It was towards this establishment that Barradell turned his gelding's nose. He climbed from the saddle, looped his rein around the peeled rack fronting the gallery and mounted the scarred steps.

He shoved the door open and walked into yellow lamplight, leaving the sounds of the street and the half-heard strains of the guitar behind.

A stocky, grey-haired man with a melancholy down-sweep of moustache and a bright watch-chain looped across a flowered vest was leaning against a counter which was piled high with almost every kind of goods that mankind could require. The only other occupant of the store was a hunched-up Papago Indian who squatted in a sleeping, blanket-wrapped bundle close to the door.

The stocky man did not alter his leaning position, but watched the gun-hung stranger stride towards him with ringing spurs.

'You're Timothy Mannix, mayor of this town?' Barradell inquired as he approached.

The grey-haired man nodded.

Barradell fished in a shirt-pocket under his buck-skin vest and produced a folded letter which he handed to Mannix. He accompanied the action with words spoken slowly and deliberately:

'My name is Smith – you sent me this letter.'

'Smith?' queried the storekeeper and mayor of Santa Rita.

'It's Smith while I'm here,' Barradell said confiden-tially, one eye on the apparently sleeping Papago by the door.

Realization dawned on Mannix as he glanced at the letter, written in his own hand.

'Oh, welcome – Mr Smith. Don't mind old Carlos, he's asleep an' he's quite trustworthy, anyway. You made it in surprisingly short time; it's good to meet you,' he extended a work-calloused hand. Barradell shook and Mannix jerked his head towards a small door at the rear of the counter.

'Come into the livin'-room, I'll fix you a meal,' he invited.

Just as they moved for the door, a whooping screech

issued from the street outside, followed by the double crack of a wildly fired six-gun. A loud, gravel-edged voice that must have been audible in Tucson bellowed:

'I'm a rantin', roarin', lone-star Texas man! I don't like Yanks, I hate Mexes an' I ain't got no time for Injuns! I ain't got no time for nothin' or nobody, but whiskey an' shootin'! Anybody want a fight, let him walk out this-away with his iron smokin'!'

Barradell swung on his heel and walked swiftly towards the door, Mannix following.

'It's Butch Albertson, warming up for a night's drinkin',' the mayor explained. 'He's a hanger-on of the Border Bunch. This kind of thing is mild compared with some of their ructions since they shot Marshal Poindexter. They're terrifying Santa Rita and the whole district around, makin' this a wide open town. All the deputies resigned after the marshal was shot down, most of 'em ran out of the country—'

His words were lost as a crackle of wild fire sounded from the street and another series of whiskey-thick rebel yells was loosed.

Barradell stood close to the door, watching the scene on the street through its small window. A mountain of a man was standing on unsteady, spraddled legs in the middle of the street, gripping a whiskey bottle in one hand and flourishing a smoking six-gun in the other. Butch Albertson was whooping that this was his night to holler and the citizenry of Santa Rita scuttled for cover.

Mannix noted the way Barradell's fingers clawed over the butt of his holstered six-gun in an absent manner as he surveyed the scene. Out on the darkened street, Albertson ceased his yelling, took a long pull at the whiskey bottle, swerved around and lurched towards an adobe cantina on the far side of the street.

'Yeah, I guess you can call that mild,' commented Barradell. 'Leastways, he didn't kill anybody!' The broad back of Albertson disappeared unsteadily through the batwing doors of the cantina.

'The wonder is that there's some of us left alive,' returned Mannix and he resumed the interrupted journey towards the back room. 'Those outlaws are takin' over this town fast an' we need someone like you badly. Marshal Poindexter was a good man, but he was shot from ambush three weeks ago. Nobody around these parts will take his badge; that's why the Law and Order Committee decided to send for you when a newly-hired hand on Charlie Riddle's Rafter R outfit said he'd lately been workin' up in Montana an' knew you were up there.'

Mannix took the newcomer into a small, neatly furnished bachelor apartment at the rear of the store and set a coffee-pot to boiling on an oil-burner. Barradell removed his hat and sat down on the chair towards which the storekeeper waved a hand.

'This Poindexter, was he Al Poindexter?' he asked levelly.

'That was him,' Mannix answered. 'A fine lawman, though some folk said he had a bad reputation up north an' gained a pardon by turnin' state's evidence against one of his outlaw partners.'

'He did,' replied Jeff Barradell coldly, 'and, just in case you haven't heard already, Mr Mannix, some people will tell you somethin' of that sort about me!'

The mayor's moustache seemed to take on a more marked degree of droopiness quite suddenly. He said:

'Oh? Well, if that's so, I guess it's your own business.'

'I guess it is – if it's so.'

Mannix pottered around in a small kitchen opening off the living-room and produced hot beans and pork in a surprisingly short time.

As Barradell ate thankfully, he asked questions.

'How long has the Border Bunch been runnin' around here?'

'Oh, a matter of about three or four months – they showed up around here just after they started operatin' along the border. They must have their roost somewhere south of here, but nobody knows where any more than they know who the boss of the outfit is or where they're goin' to show up next. They always show up here sooner or later, though, to go on a liquor spree – I guess there's more of 'em in town right now as well as Butch Albertson.'

'Yeah, an' they'll have money to sling around some, too, since they robbed the Satisfaction Mine payroll over near Tombstone recently,' Barradell mused. 'Which way do they sashay when they ride out of town?'

'South, always south. Nobody dare follow them, but maybe their hideout is south of the border. Anyway, now that Poindexter is dead, this is rapidly becoming their town. They ride around here wide open, sure that nothin' in the way of a law enforcement officer will bother 'em. We formed the Law an' Order Committee to try an' do somethin' about it an' sent for you.'

Barradell grunted. It was the same story, he thought – lawlessness running rife with no one to check it effectively. The lawless element was disporting itself brazenly in the open, making Santa Rita into another Jackson's Hole, another Deadwood or another Tombstone – a wide-open town for outlaws.

He shoved his empty plate away from him and began to fish in his shirt-pocket for the makings. Mannix watched as he rolled and lit a cigarette.

From the street, another whoop and hurrah came echoing, followed by the slam of a gun.

As if this were some awaited signal, Barradell stood up.

'Will you take the proposition we offered in the letter?' asked the mayor of Santa Rita urgently.

'Are yoy a JP, Mr Mannix?'

'Yes, but that doesn't mean much in this town any more.'

'It means you can swear me in right now,' retorted Barradell, raising his right hand as he spoke.

Mannix performed the swearing-in ceremony rapidly and Barradell responded with the neccessary 'I do'. The mayor of Santa Rita fished in his vest pocket and produced a worn marshal's star.

'It was Poindexter's,' he explained. 'I kept it on me in case you'd accept our offer.'

Barradell pinned the badge on his vest. From the street, the sounds of whooping, wild shots and the tinkle of shattering glass came.

Jeff Barradell turned about on his high heels, striding for the store with a purposeful tread.

'Where are you goin'?' asked Mannix.

'Out on the street, where a marshal belongs,' Barradell said levelly.

He hitched up his cartridge-studded holster belt as he moved into the store.

TWO

The sharp blast of a six-gun slammed out of the door-way of the cantina as Barradell was crossing the street. A wildly gyrating figure in Mexican costume came spinning out of the batwing doors, clutching an injured shoulder, teetered across the plankwalk and pitched into the dust. The gusty bellow of Butch Albertson's drunken laughter issued from the building. The sprawling Mexican squawked: 'That *Tejano*, he is crazy!'

'That's the way to treat stinkin' Mexes!' roared Albertson's voice from within. 'Put bullets in 'em an' kick 'em out of a Texan's society! Remember the Alamo! To hell with greasers!'

Jeff Barradell approached the drinking-house with a peculiar, cat-footed and stalking gait. His right hand hung poised above the butt of his Colt. Santa Rita's citizenry, scurrying from the vicinity of the cantina, stared with round-eyed wonderment at the tall man with the law badge on his vest moving towards the scene of the drunkard's disturbance.

21

He shouldered the batwings open and entered the small cantina with soft-footed speed. It was a place of narrow proportions. Its brassy lamplight, issuing from a single oil-lamp bracketed on a greasy adobe wall, was fogged by cigarillo smoke with which the blue drift of cordite haze dribbling from the mouth of Albertson's naked gun mingled.

The big Texan was standing close to the small bar, holding his six-shooter in one hand and in the act of swigging cheap whiskey from the neck of a bottle. He was far gone in drink and wavering on his feet.

In a far corner, a group of frightened Mexicans with a dark-haired girl in a brightly flowered dress among them, clustered into a rigid huddle. An old Mexican was half stooped behind the bar in fear and a bunch of hard-faced Americans in cowboy clothing leaned against the bar, grins of admiration on their ill-shaven faces. More hangers-on of the Border Bunch, thought Barradell.

A pregnant silence settled on the cantina as the stranger with the marshal's star moved through the haze of smoke, hand clawed over the gun-butt at his thigh, making a bee-line for Butch Albertson. Albertson, with his bullet head thrown back and the neck of the bottle held to his lips, did not notice Barradell's approach.

Barradell halted a mere twelve inches away from the drunken Texan.

'Get on yore cayuse an' sashay out of town, Albertson – pronto!' he ordered in an ice-cold tone.

Butch Albertson stiffened in his pose, then lowered

the bottle slowly, to regard Barradell with bleary eyes in a brutal, broken-nosed face which had not known contact with a razor for a full week. Barradell watched the rest of the American hard-cases fan out against the bar with a slow, trouble-anticipating action.

Albertson glowered at the lean newcomer as if he was something distasteful. The lamp-sheened star on Barradell's vest took his attention and he hooted a thick laugh. He dropped the bottle to the dirty boards of the floor, shattering it to splinters in a pool of eighth-rate liquor.

'What the hell have we here?' he husked in brutal amusement. 'A lawman in this town! This is damned funny!'

'Get outside an' leave town – that goes for the whole crew of you!' Barradell stated in the same flat tone. His crook-fingered hand still hovered over his holster.

Albertson's pistol was held in a downward-pointing pose.

'Who in the flames of hell,' he demanded thickly, 'might you be?'

'You can call me Smith,' Barradell retorted without emotion, 'Slim Smith. I'm marshal of this town an' I'm runnin' you out.'

'Call you Smith;' mimicked Albertson. 'If I wanted to call you anythin', *hombre*, I'd call you—'

'Shut yore mouth an' get out!' cut in Barradell. 'You're fallin' down drunk!'

Albertson persisted:

'I'd call you a lousy son of a—'

Barradell hit him hard across his whisker-bristled

mouth with the flat of his left hand, bringing a trickle of blood from a split lip.

Butch Albertson rocked back on his heels and there was an uneasy motion among the rest of the hard-cases as if each was activated by the same string.

'Outside,' ordered Barradell. 'Outside, *muy pronto!*'

'Why, you—!' spluttered Albertson. The gun in his hand moved upwards.

Barradell's drawing of his six-gun was a feat which those who witnessed were at a loss to describe after-wards. It was accomplished in a single, fluid motion of the poised hand – a fast dip down and a faster upsweep. It's hard mouth was pressed against Butch Albertson's ample stomach before he completed the upward movement with the gun he held.

'Throw that iron down, Albertson,' ordered the newly-appointed marshal. 'And, the rest of you, keep yore paws from yore hardware or Butch gets a gutful of daylight!'

Albertson's gun and his jaw dropped at one and the same time. The rest of the Border Bunch cohorts stiff-ened against the bar astonished at the eye-baffling swiftness of that gunslinger's draw.

'I'll gun you down for this!' mouthed Albertson in a croaking bluster. 'So help me, mister, whoever you are – I'll gun you down! I'll smoke this out with you—'

'Right now, you'll shut yore mouth.' Barradell said crisply, 'an' you'll do as I say. Turn around an' head out of that door. You go first, the rest of you follow, one by one. Fork yore horses an' ride. Next time you show yore noses in this town, come in sober an' go out peaceable.'

The gunless Albertson began to mutter threats under his breath; nevertheless, he turned his heavy bulk around and began to head for the batwing doors. The remaining hardcases followed him sheepishly.

Teetering drunkenly, Albertson turned his head as he neared the door.

'I'll fix you for this, Smith,' he growled.

'Try it when you're sober.' counselled Barradell grimly as he moved at the backs of the departing men.

The Mexican patrons of the cantina heaved audible sighs of relief and glanced thankfully at each other. Out on the street, news of a new marshal of Santa Rita had travelled rapidly and a knot of curious townsfolk stood in an inquisitive cluster at a respectable distance from the entrance to the cantina. The deflated hardcases moved for the group of ponies hitched at the rack close to the drinking establishment.

Barradell stood on the plank-walk, the gun still gripped in his hand, watching them mount up. In a surly bundle, they yanked their animals around and moved off southward down the single street.

There was a respectful and almost amazed silence about the onlookers, who gazed at the tall and lean stranger as if he was something newly-dropped from a distant star.

The shuffle of boots sounded at Barradell's back and a voice, with a cultured tone which seemed out of place in this setting said:

'That was smart – the way you handled them. Don't underestimate them, though – they'll be back and they'll raise hell!'

Barradell caught the taint of whiskey on the speaker's breath. He turned and saw a young man, lean-featured and with a neatly trimmed beard and sweeping moustache standing close to him.

The young man wore a frock coat, a little the worse for wear, over a yellow vest and pearl-grey trousers, both of which articles of wear looked expensive but had obviously seen better days. His hat was a black, low-crowned sombrero and a Smith & Wesson five-shooter was hung in a holster at his cartridge-decorated belt.

'Yes, sir, Marshal, they'll be back. They're as mean as rattlers with boils, those fellows. I saw your whole play over the top of the batwings and admired it greatly. I hung around in case anyone needed my services.'

'Your services?' queried Barradell. He had already sized up the young man as a gambler deep into hard times.

The bearded young man smiled. It was a hard smile. Despite his obvious youth, this man had the appearance of being unable to smile with any humour.

'Allow me to introduce myself.' he said. 'George Merriam, doctor of medicine. I'm this town's only medico – the only one in almost ninety miles, in fact.'

The doctor watched the retreating backs of Butch Albertson and his companions disappear into the dusty gloom, then he nodded towards the cantina.

'Join me in a drink, by way of welcoming you to Santa Rita?' he asked.

'Sure,' rejoined Barradell. They turned and entered the cantina.

A group of enthusiastic and voluble Mexicans surged around Barradell as he entered with Merriam. Having been shaken out of their scared poses, they wanted to press their thanks upon the new marshal of Santa Rita. Butch Albertson had been warming up to one of his ugliest anti-Mexican moods and one Latin had already received a slug in his shoulder. The intervention of the stranger with the star of a marshal on his vest had prevented the bully's fury from reaching its full spate – in which case Albertson would remember the Alamo, Goliad, San Pacinto and a dozen more Texan grievances against Mexico, taking it upon himself to clear up those old scores with bullets.

Merriam and Barradell shouldered the Mexicans aside and made their way to the bar.

'Two whiskies, Emiliano,' ordered Merriam. 'Out of the good bottle, *amigo*.'

The Mexican bartender, only just snapping out of his fright, produced a dusty bottle with a Scottish label and poured two generous glassfulls, waving away the payment proffered by the medico.

'In honour of the new marshal,' explained the barkeeper with a yellow-toothed smile.

Barradell sipped the whisky and contemplated the young medico. This man's bearing marked him out of place in this desert-edge border town. Merriam had pressed his companionship upon the newly arrived marshal and Barradell wondered why. Questions began to form in his mind. This was the territory of the mysterious, fast-swooping Border Bunch, the ruthless renegades led by some unknown master-mind. There was no telling who was friend or foe, here. No telling on whose side a young, obviously bottle-wooing medico with a smooth tongue might be.

'Some town, this,' observed Merriam after he had downed the whisky with a quick action. 'Suspended between Mexico and Arizona with nothing around it but desert – it's a devil of a place for trouble.'

Barradell considered that for a moment, wondering whether he detected a hostile warning in it.

'Most border towns are,' he answered casually.

'They don't all have outlaw crews like the Border Bunch hovering around them,' Merriam said. 'I didn't catch your name, Marshal.'

Barradell motioned for two more whiskies. He admired the poise of Doctor George Merriam. He'd had a full share of drink this night, but he knew how to hold it.

'I didn't mention it, but it's Smith,' he said slowly.

A tight smile – almost a smile of unbelief – quirked the corners of Merriam's mouth under its fringe of moustache and beard.

'The last marshal was Al Poindexter,' he answered. 'Al Poindexter who had the big six-gun reputation.'

'I've heard of him,' Barradell grunted.

'Got shot out on the desert – shot from ambush,' Merriam said.

Jeff Barradell wondered if there was a threatening note in that, too.

'That was hard; they say he was a good law-officer.'

'Wasn't always a strictly law-abiding citizen

himself,' Merriam remarked, licking the lingering dew of the whisky from his moustache.

'He was mixed up with Billy the Kid's gunnies in the Lincoln County War, if that's what you mean,' Barradell replied, gazing into the haze of tobacco smoke curtaining the cantina. 'A lot of men got mixed up in things like that, sometimes against their will. Depends where a fellow thinks his loyalty lies.'

He was surprised at the words he found his own mouth framing. It seemed that, since pinning Al Poindexter's badge to his vest, he'd taken to carrying his banner for him. He, himself, had been forced to the path of waywardness once and earned a reputation as a slick-trigger man. Maybe, he thought, it had been something like that with Al Poindexter – although Poindexter was said to have been a wanton killer and outlaw who'd taken to the path of the law after turning state's evidence against a partner of the night-trails.

What the hell! They said the same thing about him, didn't they? Barradell wondered where this seedy and drunken young medico fitted into the set-up around Santa Rita and what, if any, was his connection with the notorious Border Bunch whose hide-out and leader no one knew.

Merriam was talking again:

'Now you, Mr Smith, carry your gun like a man who's long been used to carrying one and you draw it that way, too. I saw you clear leather on Albertson – it was fast!'

Barradell was standing with his back half-presented to Merriam; he swivelled about quickly and faced the medical man squarely. The dark eyes under his black brows held a frosty bleakness.

'I wear my gun this way because I *am* used to wearin' it an' I draw it fast because I'm used to drawin' it that way, too.' It was a statement clearly intended to mark the end of the trend of the conversation. He had the distinct impression that Merriam was sounding him in an attempt to find out what lay at his back. The sharpness of his answer was lost on the drunken doctor. He asked outright:

'Where are you from?'

'Any place my horse leaves his hoofprints an' any place my boot-heels leave a trail,' answered Barradell with a hard edge to his voice.

Merriam smirked.

'Have another drink, Marshal,' he invited.

'No, thanks,' Barradell said, 'I think you've had enough, too.'

From out in the street beyond the batwing doors, the sudden tramp of hooves came and the husky voice of Butch Albertson roared:

'Come on out, Smith! Come on out here on the street an' we'll gun out our grudge!'

'Barradell stiffened up from his leaning posture against the bar.

'They're back,' declared Merriam. He said it quite philosophically, as if the occurrence was as much to be expected as morning following night. 'Got as far as the plaza, I guess, then their drunken chivalry was too much for them. They came back for a showdown!'

In the cantina, Mexicans were scuttling for the small door which led to the back room. Barradell could see nothing over the top of the batwings save the glimmer of lamplight from the window of Mannix's store across the street. He didn't need telling that Albertson was not out there alone, waiting to smoke out his grudge with a borrowed gun – the rest of his *mal hombre* drinking companions would be located at various points of the street, ready to open up on him as soon as he stepped out of the cantina.

And what of this lean, smiling man at his side? On whose side was he – would he make a move to use that Smith & Wesson on Barradell's back as the new marshal moved for the door?

'I'm waitin', Smith!' yowled Albertson. 'I'm waitin' for you to come out an' show yoreself! We'll gun it out – you an' me! Are you yeller?'

Barradell moved away from Merriam's side with a quick skip, the Colt coming into his hand with that swift draw as he did so. If he was going to take that bunch on the street, he'd have to turn his back on the unknown quantity that was Dr George Merriam, trusting to his gunfighter's sixth sense to warn him if the medico moved for his gun and the swiftness in turning about with a blazing weapon if Merriam tried to shoot.

'I'm waitin' for you, Smith! ' whooped the whiskey-thick voice from the street.

Barradell began to edge for the door, keeping out of direct line with it. With the corner of his eye, he saw Merriam's Smith & Wesson five-shot come into his hand with a surprising swiftness – almost as fast as

his own draw. He jumped about again, facing the
doctor, frozen into a gunpointing, half-crouched and
spraddle-legged pose.

Merriam was leaning against the bar, nonchalantly
as before, the five-shot in his hand.

'Don't be a fool, Smith,' he cautioned. 'Albertson
isn't out there alone. His drinking friends are with
him, probably ringing the door of this place. They'll
make a sport of it – cut you down as soon as you step
through the door. You won't stand a chance – *you*
ought to know the tactics of men of that calibre.' He
said the 'you' as if he had pierced the flimsy mask of
'Smith' and knew who and what Barradell was.

Instinctively, Barradell knew that this bearded
young man, whose drunkenness now seemed to have
have slipped from him like a cloak, was to be trusted.

The drawn-out screech of a rebel yell issued from
the street and Albertson's drawling Texas tones
demanded loudly: 'Are you comin' out, Smith, or do I
have to come in?'

Barradell resumed his move for the door. The
cantina was empty now, the frightened Mexican clien-
tele having scooted for the back room to a man.
Barradell flattened himself against the adobe wall at
the side of the door. From here, he had a sidelong view
of the street. He could not see the still-roaring
Albertson, but he saw a finger of lamplight put a
sheen on a flourished shot-gun at one corner of
Mannix's store and a dark, big-hatted silhouette edged
itself cautiously around the side of a stationary wagon
in the centre of the rutted street.

'There's two of 'em in that direction, at least,' he told himself as he contemplated the small segment of the street in view from his position against the wall.

Merriam reached up and turned down the wick of the bracketed oil-lamp, quenching the light quickly. He moved cat-footed for the single window, set in the wall on the opposite side of the door from where Barradell stood.

'I'll spot them from here,' he stated, dropping to his knees as he approached the grimy glazed aperture. Barradell appraised his movements half-conscious that he was doing so. The way he moved and the way he carried his gun made it abundantly clear that this was not the first time Dr George Merriam took a hand in gunplay. In the ill-lit cantina – light seeped into the bar-room in yellow fingers from the door of the back-room – the two men waited, Barradell close to the door, flattened against the wall, Merriam down on his knees by the window, his head raised cautiously to survey the street.

Butch Albertson bellowed: 'I'm gettin' tired, Smith – come on out an' fight!'

'Butch is standing in the middle of the street, off to the side of the cantina, so you can't see him from where you are,' Merriam reported calmly. 'Two of his friends are over at the entrance to the alley between Mannix's and the saddle-maker's store. I can just make them out, and there's another behind the water barrel outside Mannix's place.'

'And there are two more out of your line of vision,' commented Jeff Barradell, 'one with a shotgun at the far end of Mannix's gallery and the other behind a wagon in the middle of the street.'

'I can take the two at the alley-corner and the one behind the water-barrel from here,' the medico declared, 'and Butch, too.'

'No, leave Butch to me,' Barradell said grimly. 'I'll accommodate the one behind the wagon an' the one at that end of Mannix's – Butch is easy meat, he's too drunk to be dangerous.'

'Come on out an' face me, Smith, you yeller-bellied skunk!' roared Albertson. 'Come on out an' face a rantin', roarin' Texan.'

'Let's go!' snapped Barradell.

As Merriam raised the barrel of his pistol to shatter a pane of the window, Barradell, without moving from his sheltered position by the door, slammed a shot over the top of the batwings at the dark silhouette of the man by the wagon, who was well out of cover, probably enboldened by the failure of any answer to Albertson's bluster to come from the cantina: The figure gave a squawk and flopped backwards. Instantly, the white flame of the shot-gun, located over at the corner of the store opposite seared into the night and the scream of its shell echoed on the bellowing explosion. Barradell ducked backwards as the shell slapped into a corner of the cantina portal, showering dry adobe into the waves of gunsmoke.

Over at the window, the shadowy form of Merriam was systematically blasting shots through the broken glass at adversaries out of Barradell's line of vision.

A couple of hastily thrown slugs ripped into the slatted batwing doors, tearing shards of wood away. That would be Albertson, Barradell figured as he edged towards his old position by the door. Through a haze of swirling cordite smoke and drifting adobe dust, he dimly saw the shot-gun artist levelling his lamplight-sheened weapon for another shot. He triggered two slugs over the top of the batwings, saw the dim figure leap into a puppet-like dance of short duration then fall forward to the dark earth stiff as a felled tree.

More slugs, slammed from a single gun, peppered the batwings and the adobe surrounding them.

Merriam had stopped shooting. Out of the semi-darkness, his voice said, lazily: 'That's Albertson, Smith, he's on the street on his own now, you can take him without any of his pals gunning you!'

Barradell sped into action, whirling through the batwings and on to the boardwalk in a headlong run, gun pointing in exactly the direction he expected Albertson to be. He jerked to a halt on the scuffed boardwalk, standing in a crouching, gun-killer's position. Albertson was standing in the middle of the dark street, teetering drunkenly. He yelled in a panic-edged voice as Barradell slithered to a standstill:

'No! Smith, my gun's empty! My gun's empty!'

'Drop it! ' snarled Barradell. 'Drop it in the dirt, or I'll drop you!'

Butch Albertson allowed his borrowed six-gun to slither from his fingers. The ranting, roaring Texan was now quaking before the wicked snout of

Barradell's Colt, his yellow streak on full view for all
Santa Rita to see. Jeff Barradell advanced on him
slowly. Albertson watched, round-eyed and swaying
drunkenly. His whiskey-fuzzed intellect had not yet
taken in the fact that two streams of death-dealing
lead had crackled out of the cantina at the same time,
disintegrating the gun-trap he had laid for the new
marshal in a matter of a few seconds.

'So you're a rantin', roarin' Texan, eh Butch?'
Barradell smiled grimly. 'You were goin' to fight it out
man to man with me – only there wouldn't have been
much of me left to fight by the time yore planted
gunnies look me as I stepped out of that shebeen.'

Albertson was thoroughly cowed now and for the
second time that night he found the new marshal of
Santa Rita pressing his six-shooter close to his centre
shirt-button. Barradell's tone took on a harder edge.

'You're in with this Border Bunch, ain't you, Butch?'

Large expanses of white became visible in Butch
Albertson's wide eyes.

'No – I don't know anythin' about 'em!'

Barradell quirked a grim smile.

'You know who the big man is an' where they hang
out?'

'No, I don't know anythin' about 'em, I tell you.'

Interested spectators were appearing from cover
along various points of the street, standing around to
witness the humiliation of loud-mouthed Butch
Albertson, by this stranger with the badge of the late
Marshal Poindexter.

'You're a liar, Butch;' he told Albertson coldly. 'Where do you live?'

'On a waterhole over on Conquistadore Rim, I'm prospectin' over that way, got a cabin there.'

'You're still a liar, Butch. You're no prospector, you got cowman written all over you. If you're livin' on a waterhole, you're squattin' on it, keepin' it for rustler use. You're a Border Bunch man, Butch, an' I know it. I ought to arrest you for shootin' at that Mexican an' for tryin' to assassinate me, but I'll give you a chance to ride out of town so you can tell yore Border Bunch *amigos* an' the big man, whoever he is, that Santa Rita has a new marshal an' no one is goin' to bushwhack him. You can tell em all that this town is goin' peaceful; it won't become another Jackson, Deadwood or Tombstone for *mal hombres* of their kind to throw their weight around in. Where's yore horse?'

Albertson nodded towards a hitch-rack.

'Turn around an' walk for it,' Barradell told him, motioning with his gun. At the horse, Barradell kept the Colt prodded in the big Texan's back while deftly snatching a Winchester out of the saddle-boot.

'I'll confiscate this, Butch, you ain't a fit person to carry firearms.'

'You can't do that,' protested Albertson. 'I need a gun for protection. Suppose I meet wild critters on the trail!'

'Tell 'em you're a rantin', roarin' Texas man an' they'll turn tail an' run for miles,' Barradell grated. 'Now climb into yore saddle an' ride. Don't forget to tell yore Border Bunch friends what I told you!'

Butch Albertson swung his bulk into the saddle, bestowed a glare on the new marshal of Santa Rita who slapped a hard hand over the animal's rump, sending it off down the street at a brisk trot.

'Keep clear of this town in future, Butch, an' tell yore friends to do the same!' Barradell yelled after the departing man.

The motley citizenry of Santa Rita turned admiring eyes on the lean man who had made his presence in town felt so strongly.

The dark-coated figure of Dr George Merriam came ambling across from the cantina, smiling his humourless smile.

'I guess Santa Rita knows it's got itself a marshal now – er – Smith,' he commented. Barradell grunted, watching the dust raised by Albertson's horse cloud into the gloom down by the plaza. Merriam put a subtle inflection on 'Smith' again and Barradell reflected that he either knew exactly who he was or considered the name he had assumed too common to be that of an obvious gunfighter with a 'reputation'. On the heels of that reflection came the memory of Merriam's fast draw and his obvious gunfighter tactics in the cantina. Doctor he might have been, but when he went into action against Albertson's positioned gunhands, he moved like a seasoned gunslinger. There was much mystery about this semi-sober, hard-smiling, bearded and youthful medico, but Barradell was grateful for his aid in fighting off Albertson's friends.

'I'll guess it was a fair start to makin' them rowdies realize there's some law in this town,' he told the medico. 'I'm obliged to you, Merriam, there was no call for you to stick yore nose into my fight.'

Merriam gave him a brittle smile; when he spoke, there was an edge of something like sarcasm in his voice:

'On the contrary, marshal, it's the duty of every law-abiding citizen to aid peace-officers in their duty – and I'm a law-abiding man.' He nodded a goodnight and made off into the darkness. Barradell watched his retreating back; he was at a loss to understand Merriam. He was bitter and sardonic, in spite of his youth, obviously fond of the bottle and a fast man with a gun.

Barradell turned around and mounted the gallery of the general store owned by Timothy Mannix, shouldering aside the townsfolk who cluttered about him.

Bronze lamplight bloomed from the window in the door and touched the star on his buckskin vest – Al Poindexter's badge. Barradell had never known Poindexter save by reputation, the reputation of a slick-trigger man whose fame travelled along the frontier. It was a spotty reputation – there were few lawmen who didn't possess such reputations. Nevertheless, Al Poindexter had been a good marshal in this town, they said; and he'd been gunned down from ambush. Barradell found himself thinking of him as a symbol – perhaps a man like himself, trying to live down the past by serving the law.

He fingered the law-star as he entered the store.

'Maybe I'm just the natural choice to follow in Poindexter's tracks,' he thought grimly, remembering his own reputation.

THREE

Timothy Mannix clapped Barradell on the back as he entered the store.

'Good work,' he praised. 'That bunch of rowdies knows we have a marshal in town now!'

'Yeah,' murmured Barradell, 'but I was helped by your doctor. That ruckus could never have been settled without his help.'

Mannix pursed his whisker-fringed lips in obvious disapproval at the mention of Merriam.

'Merriam's almost as much a liability to this town as he is an asset,' the storekeeper pronounced. 'He drinks too much, gambles too much an' he's fond of settlin' arguments with bullets.'

Barradell saw for the first time that a man and a girl were standing outside the ring of light cast from the lamp on the raftered ceiling. The man was garbed in dark broadcloth, a wide-brimmed sombrero and cowboy boots and he was nearing fifty. The girl, standing close to his side, was slender, raven-haired and possessed an almost classical beauty. She wore her hair braided at the nape of her neck in the fashion of the period and her riding-jacket, skirt and tooled Spanish boots were fashionable without being flamboyant.

'Mr Smith, this is Miss Riddle and her father, Charlie Riddle, owner of the Rafter R ranch and chairman of our Law and Order Committee,' introduced Mannix.

Barradell moved towards the rancher and his daughter, lifting his sombrero and waiting to see if the girl would offer him her hand. She did not, but gave him a curt nod. The cattleman extended a hard hand and shook Barradell's firmly.

'Smith, eh?' he said. There was a knowing gleam in his eye.

'Smith,' nodded Barradell.

'Alicia and I came into town just as the shooting started,' Riddle told him. 'We watched it from here, the whole thing. We saw Butch Albertson come back after you hazed him out and start planting his friends around the street. I was making ready to take care of those on the gallery here myself when you and Merriam opened up and rendered any action from my quarter unnecessary.'

He flipped back his broadcloth coat and slapped a hand on a Colt .44 holstered at his middle.

'Much obliged for the thought,' Barradell heard himself mutter. Behind the words, his brain was active in appraising Charlie Riddle and registering dislike. He didn't like the rancher's stilted fashion of speech for one thing and, while he had the tight grip and the general appearance of a clean cowman, there was something deep in him that put Barradell on his guard.

'It's a good thing you answered our plea, Mr Smith,' Riddle was saying. 'Good lawmen are hard to find around here these days and we need a good lawman hereabouts if the country's going to be safe so a man can flourish and make money.'

It was the last sentence that caused Barradell to realize what it was he mistrusted in the rancher. He was a money man. He was made of the stuff that produced little range-lords; he was of the kind that wanted to become a man of power in this region – replacing the old-time *hidalgos* who ran the show when this territory was part of New Spain. The real-ization brought distasteful memories of a similar type of man in his native Nevada – a grasping man who turned his gun-heavy crew of wranglers loose on the little horse-ranch Barradell's father was trying to build up and razed it to the ground. Such a man as that was Charlie Riddle, or such a man he could become: the kind of man who made Jeff Barradell, aged eighteen, follow the philosophy that the little man hadn't a chance against the big one unless he shoved his back hard against the wall and faced the world with a bucking six-shooter.

'Good lawman or otherwise, I owe a lot to Dr Merriam for helping me out in that fracas,' he answered slowly. He tried not to show his dislike of the rancher, but the aversion lingered deep in him. Mannix seemed genuine enough as the rest of the town's Law and Order Committee, whoever they were, probably were also. He knew, however, that Charlie Riddle didn't really give a damn about law and order. He saw Barradell only as a gun-marshal, a six-shooter specialist to be hired to clean up the country so he could grow rich and fat and establish a cattle-empire, probably by kicking the smaller men around. And if the gun-marshal, the lawman with the spotty reputation, the man whose trigger-skill was bought, was shot, another one could be bought – there was bound to be one somewhere. It was all as simple as that to a money man.

Mention of Merriam caused the cattleman's brows to bracket down over his nose angrily.

'Merriam's a sot and a fool,' grunted Riddle. 'He's running a brilliant brain to seed – sometimes he's so drunk he can't do his duty as a doctor. He shouldn't get into that state, doctoring's his business – that's what he's paid for!'

Barradell nodded without the rancher knowing he was nodding not in agrement with his words but in confirmation of his inward conviction. With Riddle, it was all money: there were no other values in the world.

Alicia Riddle turned her head sharply to face her father. Her fine brow was puckered into a crease of anger and her dark eyes glittered. It was obvious that she was holding her tongue only by a strong effort of will and, with one of those sudden flashes of realization that are sometimes given to a man, Jeff Barradell saw that this girl was in love with the drunken, lead-throwing young medico. It was either love or pity, he reflected, for there was something heart-tearing in watching a man of intellect and accomplishment allowing the bottle to master him in a dirty, fly-bitten border town.

Riddle did not fail to note his daughter's flash of anger, but turned his head away from her deliberately.

'Have you moved into the marshal's quarters yet, Mr Smith?' he asked.

'Not yet,' Barradell responded. 'Other considerations have pressed on me kind of hard since I reached town.'

'There's a cosy set of living quarters right behind the jail,' the rancher told him, 'if you have no objections to sleeping in a dead man's bed, that is.'

'None,' Barradell said, 'just so long as no one has any ideas about trying to make me share his grave.'

A silence descended on the group in which only Riddle moved, fingering his wind-burned chin. Jeff Barradell was conscious of the cattleman's daughter contemplating him, not quite looking down her straight, Grecian nose, but eyeing him with a distinct haughtiness. He didn't think he could take to her any more than he could to her father. She reminded him of some of the city girls he'd met on a trip to Chicago once: they thought they had some kind of squatters' rights on the world and everyone in it because no one up-ended them and spanked their tail-boards when they were youngsters.

Barradell broke the silence by pushing the subject of the late marshal of Santa Rita.

'How was Poindexter bushwhacked?' he asked. 'Rumour says he was a hard man to surprise.'

Riddle went on rubbing his chin slowly, almost calculatingly, Barradell thought.

'He was surprised all right,' the rancher answered, 'shot out of the saddle close to the edge of my holdings. He was investigating after some cattle was run off my ranges. We found him three days after he was first missed. The coyotes and buzzards had been at him; he wasn't a pretty sight.'

Barradell grunted. He didn't need telling that any corpse that had lain three days on the edges of the desert rims as prey for the wild things of the wide land was not a pretty sight by the time of its discovery. So that was how they treated lawmen around here: bushwhacked them and left them for the coyotes and buzzards. He began to see Al Poindexter as a symbol again – the symbol of his kind of man, the gunman trying to cover over the bullet-pocked traces, crying out for vengeance from a bushwhack grave.

'How big is your law and order organization?' Barradell asked.

'Only six members,' Mannix told him.

'Not a powerful lot to buck against an outfit like the Border Bunch,' the gunfighter observed.

'It's a start,' Riddle put in. 'The government doesn't seem to be interested in sending United States marshals out here, so it's up to us to protect our interests ourselves.' He made a flourish that seemed entirely synthetic to Barradell. 'With a hired gun,' he added, almost without realizing he'd said it. Riddle

stared at him hard, the thick brows coming down over
his nose once more.

A disconcerting thought began to worm into
Barradell's mind. They wanted him only for his gun-
skill, these people of Santa Rita; for all they cared, he
could go to hell after he'd cleaned up the town of their
enemies. He began to wonder whether, for all his
supposedly spotty reputation, they were worthy of
him. Riddle, at least, was a money man – the very kind
that would have him hounded out of the vicinity once
his hired gun made the territory safe for the Rafter R
rancher to prosper.

The thought stayed with him as he bade a goodnight to Mannix, Riddle and his daughter. It persisted
as he legged his way across the dark and quiet street
to open up the jail building with the key the mayor
gave him and it was still there as he surveyed the
small living-room at the rear of the jail.

It had a table, a chair and a small bed, the position
of which revealed the workings of the late Al
Poindexter's gunfighter's mind. It was placed in such
a position as to make it impossible for an assassin to
fire from the single, high-placed window.

Somebody, possibly Mannix, had made the place
ready for him, providing the bed with clean sheets.
Barradell lay on top of the bed after dumping his
warsack on the table and unshucking his gun-gear. He
laid it on the floor where a hand dropped from the bed
would contact the butt of the Colt at once.

He fumbled in his shirt-pocket and produced the
makings, rolled a smoke and allowed his saddle-

wearied bones to ache out their stiffness.

Well, he was here and he'd taken their gun-marshal's job – whether they were worth risking his life for or not. And no one could say they didn't know he was in town. That run-in with Albertson and his gun-cronies had seen to that. He fell to thinking of the strange, gun-prodding medico, George Merriam, and wondered what the sardonic young man was running away from – whatever it was, it hadn't prevented the doctor from unleathering his gun and throwing slugs into his fight. For all that, Merriam was still an unknown quantity – he didn't know how he stood in relation to the mysterious renegade outfit, the Border Bunch – for, according to Mannix, Albertson and his cronies were merely hangers-on of the outlaw crew. They could have been personal enemies of the doctor's while his loyalty lay with the outlaw gang proper. Barradell was discounting no possibility.

In the wreaths of tobacco smoke drifting up to the grimed ceiling, he seemed to picture his predecessor, Al Poindexter, a man he'd never seen, but one whose gun-reputation was big but none-too-shiny. Maybe Poindexter had been his kind of man – trying to buck down his lead-slinging past by wielding a law-gun.

In which case, he owed the bushwhacked man, whose bed he now occupied, something. Poindexter was his kindred spirit. Santa Rita, scared out of its wits, took him on as gun-marshal and, when bushwhacker lead dropped him from his saddle, the town looked around frantically for another of his ilk.

Well, Santa Rita had found one. One who'd throw

some lead on behalf of Poindexter.

And no backshooter would drop this one from his saddle.

FOUR

Bull Claffin angled his horse down to the flat under Conquistadore Rim shortly after dawn. The big Texan was not a notably brave man and he rode south of Tombstone in defiance of Barradell's warning with the constant fear that Barradell would pounce upon him from behind every rock. He came at length to the scrub-guarded waterhole close to which Butch Albertson had his cabin.

The cabin was of timber hewn from the wooded lower slopes of the rim, a small structure from which a tin stovepipe slanted against the dawn-tinged sweeps of the desert sky backing it. Albertson's horse was tethered in a small lean-to and the forepart of the cabin was littered with trash which spoke of the occupant's untidy mode of life. Empty cans and bottles were scattered with an abandon telling of Butch Albertson's custom of hurling them from the door as he finished with them.

There was a silence on the place as Claffin reigned in, pacing his bronc over the hoof-tramped and fouled track of cattle that had been driven towards the shoulder of the rim after watering at the *tinaja*. The burly Texan swung his weight down from the saddle and shoved open the warped door of the building. His equally burly fellow Texan was stretched out on a narrow bunk, breathing heavily in his drunken sleep; one thick arm, clad in dirty red flannel, was hanging limply over the side of the bunk, the huge hand curled against the floor. Albertson snorted and grunted as the edge of the winter-keened air entered with Claffin, but he continued to breath heavily, until Claffin shook him roughly.

Albertson came to wakefulness, clawing for the holstered six-gun hanging from the bunk-post at his head and uttering a confused gurgle.

'Take it easy,' counselled Claffin quickly. 'Ain't no need for you to go grabbin' yore iron! It's me – Claffin!'

Albertson yanked his big frame, clad in a grimy red flannel undershirt, into a sitting position and glared at the other with dulled eyes.

'What the hell're you doin' here?' he demanded throatily.

'On my way into the hole to see the boss,' Claffin replied. 'You got any coffee? I been ridin' most of the night an' I'm blamed cold.'

The befuddled Albertson jerked his head towards the still-glowing stove.

'Fill the pot at the waterhole an' make coffee yoreself,' he said.

Claffin moved to the stove and picked up the blackened coffee-pot.

'Got news for the boss,' he mentioned. 'That Barradell – Jeff Barradell, that was marshal of Comanche Peak in Texas – headed out of Tombstone for Santa Rita yesterday. Bet you the law an' order crowd are puttin' him in as marshal. The man on the bunk stiffened, his beard-fuzzed jaw dropping open.

'Barradell!' he echoed. 'So that's who he is! I knew he was a reputation man an' no Smith!' The words were gurgled half to himself. 'Jeff Barradell – hell!'

Bull Claffin paused in mid-stride as he headed for the door with the coffee-pot in his hand.

'Yeah, Smith is the name he's goin' under – have you come across him?'

'I'll say I have. Had a run-in with him last night. He was fast on the draw an' ran me an' a bunch of the boys out of town. We went back to fix his wagon an' that blasted sawbones, Merriam, threw his gun into the fight. Walt Peaslee, Joe Calton, Clip Orrel, Dago Quetzl an' Ferd Weisser was all shot dead. He's one hell of a slug-thrower, that Barradell an' with Merriam backin' him up, it was murder!'

'I know it,' Claffin told him. 'I've seen Barradell in action. Did the law an' order crew make him marshal?'

'Yeah, he was wearin' a star an' it looks like he aims to keep our kind out of Santa Rita!'

'He's the one that'll do it,' growled Claffin, ' 'less the boss fixes him quick.'

'Just one man,' countered Albertson, 'that ain't nothin' to fight!' The words were spoken without conviction for the big Texan was thinking of the ignominy with which he'd been hoofed out of town the previous night.

'There's bullion rollin' all around Tombstone an' Bisbee,' Claffin mentioned, changing the subject as he prepared his coffee. 'Big shipment due out of Bisbee day after tomorrow that should be worth our attention. Better'n runnin' off cows, leastways the cows they rear on these desert ranges. There ain't enough feed around here to hang meat on a longhorn's ribs the way Texas graze does!'

'That what the boss sent you over that direction for – to take a look at what was worth takin'?' Albertson inquired.

'Yeah, that was where I saw Barradell, an' he saw me. He knew me from Texas, told me he'd shoot me if he saw me south of Tombstone.'

'How did he know you're in with the Border Bunch?'

'Just guessin', I suppose,' Claffin said. He shuddered. 'It ain't funny bein' told you'll be shot on sight by that guy!'

Claffin duly finished the coffee, walked from the shack and climbed into his saddle. He took his bronc south-westward at a steady walk, bringing the animal within a couple of miles of the edge of Rafter R holdings and angling down on to the desert sink country where cattle could find no graze. His way took him through stands of long-armed saguaro and thick clustered huajillo.

Eventually, as the rising dawn flooded the wide sky with brilliant light, he came to a tract of red sand, flattening away to a sheer-sided sandstone wall. Claffin took his weary horse across the sand, entered a narrow cleft in the towering rock wall and followed a snaking and rock-strewn course between sheer-rearing walls, narrowing the cloudless desert sky to a sliver of sun-touched blue. The shaly ground over which Claffin paced his mount was cattlefouled, telling of the passage of much beef on the hoof through this narrow gully.

A rocky arch opened in one wall, a wide hole worn by long-ago water erosion. Into this turned the hoofpocks of the cattle which had been driven along the gully and following them, went Bull Claffin. A ride through a short but twisting tunnel brought him into a box canyon where stunted live-oaks grew and a sparse scrub dotted the floor. A waterhole was off to one side, reflecting the light of the sun and guarded by struggling greenery.

Close to the waterhole stood a number of men, while others were squatting on their heels beside camp-fires from which the aroma of coffee and bacon in the skillets drifted. Bedrolls were spread untidily on the ground. A half-erected cabin of hewn timber, standing close to a far wall of the canyon gave the promise that these inhabitants of the secret place would soon be done with sleeping under the frost-polished stars of winter-edged nights.

Claffin unsaddled his big frame close to one of the fires. The hard-faced men around it nodded to him and the Texas cow-thief sniffed the frying bacon appreciatively.

The men around the fire would, to a man who knew his outlaws, say a man such as Jeff Barradell, have proved worthy of contemplation. Here were men who were no newcomers to villainy, whose names had appeared in the printing-ink of reward dodgers many times and in many locations: Swede Larsen, gunman; Lafe Channing, train robber; Gent Grex, gunslinging gambler, and others whose reputations as lawbreakers were known throughout the southwest.

'Where's the boss?' inquired Claffin.

Lafe Channing jerked his head towards a second fire some distance away close to which a black-garbed man was squatting, eating bacon and beans from a tin platter. Claffin approached him.

The leader of this notorious Border Bunch was a tall man, a fact which was evident even as he crouched by the fire. His black broadcloth clothing was of a smart cut and singular neatness for this setting and a wide-brimmed sombrero topped his dark, glowering features. He wore a pair of holster-belts buckled across his middle and the pearlhandled Colt .45s, nestling in the tooled leather of the tied down holsters, showed the meticulous maintenance of the man who lived by his guns. The overall appearance of this man whom the Border Bunch *bandidos* called 'the boss' was even more dandified than that of Gent Grex, the cold blooded killer who was said to raise his carefully brushed hat every time he shot a man which, with Grex, was usually in the back.

The boss glowered up from his breakfast.

'Well?' he demanded. 'What have you got to say?'

'Got news for you,' Claffin began, 'Barradell's in town an' that law an' order crowd has made him marshal.'

'I know it,' the outlaw leader grunted edgily. 'And I know what your Texas cow-snatchin' friend, Albertson, an' his drunken partners got themselves into last night. They got what was comin' to them, buckin' against Barradell an' that sawbones. If I didn't want you empty-headed beef-stealers to watch the waterholes an' run the cattle out of this country, I'd see the whole bunch of you in hell! Swede was in town last night an' he saw the whole play. Albertson an' his partners acted plumb empty-headed!'

'Swede Larsen was in town an' he didn't throw his gun in against Merriam an' Barradell?' exclaimed Claffin.

'Of course he didn't, he used his head. It wasn't the Border Bunch's fight – it was brought on by Albertson an' his loud Texas brag. They wanted to work up some hell-raisin' – an' they got it!' The outlaw leader's voice was cold and grating. 'What'd you see around Tombstone?'

'Got to hear about a load of bullion due out of Bisbee for Tucson the day after tomorrow – should make a tolerable haul.'

The leader of the Border Bunch stroked his blue-jowled features thoughtfully. 'Yes, we could lift that easy enough, I guess,' he mused. 'Jump the wagons on the Tucson trail, haze off over the desert with the load and bring it here into the hole, then take it over into Mexico the way we usually do. Yeah, bullion is better merchandise for the Border Bunch than beeves, since we don't have to rely on broken-down cow-snatchers like you an' Albertson an' his late pals to grab it for us.'

FIVE

Jeff Barradell rose early, washed his face in cold water drawn from the well in the plaza of Santa Rita and prepared a breakfast from the remains of his travelling provisions.

Then, with his gun buckled on, he stood at the door of the jail and surveyed the street. It was sun-washed and quiet with only one or two Mexican women over by the well, as yet. Someone, probably the local undertaker, whoever he was, had removed the bodies of those killed in the previous night's gunfight from the street.

Barradell returned to the cramped living quarters at the rear of the jail and began to tidy his bunk and clean up in general. He noticed droppings of red sand here and there around the room – sand of a peculiar redness which was alien to the dust of Santa Rita. It looked as if the previous occupant of the small room – Al Poindexter – had a quantity of this sand on his boots sometime shortly before he was bushwhacked and it had dropped as he walked about his apartment.

He tidied the floor then walked off along the street towards a livery stable he'd noted the night before. Here, he bought feed for his gelding, stabled at the back of the *caliboza*. As he walked to the livery stable and again as he humped the sack of feed back to his quarters, he was aware of the eyes of those on the rapidly livening street regarding him. Some stares were admiring, some dubious, some, from the law-resenting element of any border town, were definitely unfriendly.

Later in the morning, he decided to make a sortie of the land in the immediate vicinity of Santa Rita and rode unobtrusively out of town, heading in a westward direction. An hour of heading the gelding at a steady pace brought him to a belt of graze where he saw long-horns branded Rafter R and little more than a further hour of riding saw the pastures falling away at his back and the wide, arid sweeps of the desert before him.

Out of the flattening wilderness rose a long wall of suntouched red sandstone with a carpet of even redder sand spread before it.

Barradell yanked the gelding to a halt on a humped rise and regarded the stretch of sand, remembering the droppings of sand of that self-same redness he'd found on the floor of the living-quarters at the rear of the Santa Rita jail. He thumped the animal's ribs with his knees, taking it down the slope so he might have a closer view of the tract of sand.

Down on the flat under the towering red sandstone wall, he dismounted and, squatting on the ground, took a sample of the sand between his fingers. It had the same redness and the same coarseness as that he found on the floorboards of the living-quarters back in town. But what did that prove — only that Al Poindexter had walked around here at some time shortly before his death. Then, again, the sand deposited on the floor back at the jail might have come from some other source — it was certainly unusual, but that did not mean it was unique.

But, if Poindexter had been sufficiently interested in this spot to dismount and walk around here so that he got the sand on to his boots, why had he been interested?

Something to do with the Border Bunch?

Barradell's thoughts were disrupted by the far-carrying clink of a horseshoe on rock. Still squatting on the red sand, he glanced quickly upwards and saw the back of a big rider on a bronc, cresting a rise over to the north. Although the mounted man was a considerable distance off, the clear wilderness air carried the sound of the clinking shoe as if the sound occurred only a matter of yards from Barradell.

Barradell saw only the disappearing back of the big rider as he went over the hump and down the other side, but the brief glance was enough for him to recognise the man as Bull Claffin.

Claffin — headed north out of nowhere!

'By grab,' growled Jeff Barradell through clenched teeth, 'I warned that *hombre* I'd shoot him on sight if I saw him south of Tombstone! What the hell is he doin' down here on the desert?'

He leaped into the saddle of his gelding and rowelled the animal off across the tract of red sand in the direction of the hump over which the big Texas rustler had headed. At the top of the rise, he saw Bull Claffin, legging his bronc down to a rock-studded flat. Claffin turned his head sharply, saw the lean rider coming down after him, rowelled his spurs into his bronc's hide with his legs working like pistons.

'Stop, Claffin!' yelled Jeff Barradell as his gelding went half-slithering down the rise in a cloud of risen dust. Through the swirl of dust, he saw Claffin make a move for his gun and grabbed for his own six-shooter as the big rider turned in his saddle with his gun in hand. The gun barked just as Barradell's weapon was coming clear of leather and the marshal of Santa Rita feft the stinging slash of the bullet as it zipped into the fabric of his left shirt-sleeve, tearing a wound in the flesh of his arm.

Cursing inwardly, Barradell clenched his teeth against the sharp pain of the wound in his arm, saw Bull Claffin spur-punishing his mount across the dusty flat in a swirling, gritty haze. The marshal of Santa Rita fired but, even as he did so, he saw Bull Claffin's horse stumble and slither to the ground, its rider hurtling from the saddle. Spurring his gelding over the rock-studded flat, Barradell pulled rein in the dust-hung air. Claffin was lying motionless on the ground while his bronc rolled on its back with a hind leg obviously broken.

Coming out of his saddle, Barradell studied the situation. The horse, in its headlong run, had collided with one of the rocks, half-buried in dry shale and Bull Claffin appeared to have struck his head on yet another rock. The Texan was sprawled in the hot shale, quite unconscious.

Barradell assessed the plight of the bronc with one glance. There was nothing for it but to shoot the stricken animal and the marshal did so, placing the bullet square in its forehead. He crouched beside the motionless form of Claffin and dashed water from his canteen into the Texas man's face. A quiver of involuntary muscles shook Claffin's features, but he remained unconscious.

'All right,' the marshal told the senseless man, 'I'll tote you back to town the way you are!'

The flesh wound in Barradell's left arm made handling Claffin's bulk difficult, but the marshal managed to hump the big man over the fore part of his saddle after some struggling. Claffin's hat had came off as he was thrown from the bronc and the contact with the rock had cut an ugly gash in his head.

Barradell headed the double-burdened animal back towards Santa Rita and rode at the smartest pace he could coax from the gelding. The wound in his arm ached dully and questions ran through his head. Claffin was riding around this region, going somewhere – or coming from somewhere, and the marshal was willing to gamble on his activities being connected with those of the Border Bunch. He'd find out just what the Texan's game was when he came round, he reflected.

Moving the gelding steadily onward, he eventually

reached the edge of the desert-ranges whereon the Rafter R stock grazed. The sunshine was bright, but not without the weakness of winter and the wind that riffled the grazeland had the sting of the year's end in it. The rip Bull Claffin's bullet had torn into his upper arm was aching continuously. Barradell topped a rise and reflected that he must have varied from the direction he took when leaving town. For, from here, where the grama grass provided good feed for the cattle and made a contrast to the arid land he had so recently left at his back, he could see the toy-like cluster of a ranch-house and its outbuildings down on a verdant flat.

'Must be Riddle's Rafter R,' he told the unconscious man draped over his gelding's neck. 'No reason why I shouldn't stop off there, give my cayuse a rest an' clean up this wound.'

He took the double-burdened gelding down off the risetop, reached the flat and turned its nose in a direct line for the Rafter R. As he neared the house and its high barns, he appraised the well-kept appearance of the ranch headquarters. No struggling rancher's place this, he reflected. It had the brand of prosperity on it, a thriving spread – the place of a powerful money-man, he thought with distaste. Maybe Riddle made it prosperous because he ground down the smaller ranchers, the way his father had been ground down back in Nevada.

Barradell paced the weary gelding into the ranch-yard and angled across its dusty width, making for the galleried house, made of stuccoed adobe on Spanish pattern.

Over in a small, open-fronted shed, a cowhand was mending a set of harness and he stuck his big-hatted head out of the structure in an inquisitive fashion as he caught sight of the strange rider with the limp human bundle across his horse. Likewise, a Chinese face protruded from the door of what was obviously the cook's galley and watched Barradell with slanted eyes.

The marshal yanked rein close to the steps giving on to the gallery and heard a surprised, feminine voice say:

'Who are you – and what do you want?'

Barradell turned his head and saw a dark-haired girl coming along the gallery. At first he thought she was Alicia, Riddle's daughter, but saw that she was slightly smaller and, while she had something of Alicia Riddle's classic beauty, her nose was just a little tip-tilted, her eyes considerably larger and her mouth less hard than Alicia's. She wore a sweeping gown of blue in the 'hour-glass' shape of the period.

Barradell was acutely aware of his dusty appearance as the girl stood still on the gallery of the ranch-house, regarding him with bewilderment. He swept off his sombrero, feeling singularly awkward.

'I'm the marshal of Santa Rita, ma'am, they call me Slim Smith. I'm on my way to town with this man and wondered if I might stop here awhile to give my horse a blow an' clean up a wound in my arm.'

'Oh,' exclaimed the girl. 'I heard my sister and father speak of you.' She directed her gaze on the limp form of Bull Claffin.

'What's the matter with him? Is he dead?' she inquired.

'No, just gave his head a severe crack when his horse threw him.'

There was a stiff silence in which he still sat his saddle, not having been invited to dismount. Out of the door of the house came Charlie Riddle. The rancher stood on the gallery next to his daughter, contemplating Barradell and his prisoner with eyes that jerked wide open at the first instant of seeing them. Barradell did not fail to notice the brief reflection of displeasured surprise that flashed across Riddle's face.

'I'm takin' this man into town, Mr Riddle,' he explained to the owner of the Rafter R. 'I wondered if you'd mind if I rested my horse and cleaned a wound in my arm — also the wound in his head.'

'Sure,' agreed Charlie Riddle, coming down from the gallery. There was a brittle edge to his voice and the lawman had the impression that Riddle's agreement was given with a grudge.

'What happened to him?' Riddle asked as Barradell came off the back of his mount.

'His horse threw him when I was chasin' him. He hit his head on a rock. I'm takin' him in for questionin'. I knew him in Texas where he used to steal cows an' I suspect him of bein' mixed up with the Border Bunch.' He watched the rancher's face closely as he made this last statement. There was no visible reaction.

'You do, eh,' murmured Charlie Riddle, eyeing the

unconscious man slumped over the fore of the saddle. 'Take him across into the bunkhouse and we'll look at the injury to his head.' The rancher turned towards the open-fronted shed in which the cowhand was busy. 'Hey, Ed,' he hailed, 'come over and help us.'

The wrangler left the harness gear he was repairing and bowlegged across the yard.

The slender, dark-haired girl came down off the gallery.

'Come inside the house,' she invited. 'I'll attend to your arm while father and Ed take him across to the bunkhouse.' Her eyes were very blue, an unusual combination with hair so dark as hers, thought Barradell. He was aware of a hard light in them; for some reason, this slight girl did not feel particularly friendly towards him.

Barradell went up the gallery steps, following the girl while the rancher and cowhand carried the still unconscious Claffin over to the bunkhouse. He followed the blue-gowned girl into a living-room comfortably furnished for that period and location. There were comfortable armchairs with antimacassars draped over their backs, vases of flowers, velvet curtains at the window and a general cosiness which spoke of the woman's touch.

The rancher's daughter motioned the marshal to a chair while she moved briskly to a chest of drawers and produced a medicine-kit.

Barradell, conscious of his trail-dust and incongruous range-outfit, sat on the extreme edge of the soft upholstery.

The girl left the room for a few seconds and returned with a basin of hot water. She rolled up the bullet-slashed sleeve of Barradell's shirt and began to clean out the bloodcrusted bullet-furrow in the fleshy part of his upper arm. Her hands were cool and her touch light. She carried out the cleaning of the wound, dressing it with iodine and finally bandaging the arm with a chilly detachment.

Securing the bandage, she said:

'That should be all right in a few days, Marshal Barradell.' It was a cold, flat statement and the use of his correct name caused Jeff Barradell to start.

'Smith,' he stated with equal chilliness. 'The name's Slim Smith.'

The dark-haired girl was standing close to him, packing the medicine-kit back into its box, She looked square into his eyes with her frank, blue-eyed gaze. There was something in those eyes that added up to undisguised contempt.

'No. It's Barradell – Jeff Barradell, the gunfighter! The whole of this country knows who you are since you arrived – news travels fast hereabouts. You're the only kind of man they dare ask to hold down the job of marshal of Santa Rita – a gunman with a killer-reputation, one who turned a partner over to the law so he'd earn a pardon for himself!' The words came tumbling from her pretty red lips, bringing a deep stab into Barradell's pride.

Strange he should feel that hurt so acutely on hearing this from the girl. They were the words he knew men said behind his back because they hadn't the courage to say them to his face. He'd known for long enough what men said of him but, now he heard the words spoken – and by this slender girl – they stung with a deep-reaching pain.

'So you heard that,' he commented calmly.

'Yes, I heard that – all of this county has heard it and everyone knows who you are. That Smith name doesn't fool anyone!'

'If I am Jell Barradell, what's your grudge against me?' he asked.

'Just the grudge I have against all gunfighters. I don't like them for what they are. I don't like a man who chooses to make his living by hiring out his gun!'

'Maybe some men get that way without choice in the matter,' he answered. 'It could be that circumstances make a man a gunslinger just like circumstances make another a prosperous rancher.'

There was a hidden barb in the statement that made the girl arch down her dark brows.

'You mean men like my father?' she demanded. Barradell thought, grudgingly, that a man had to give her credit for fighting. She'd yanked him into this argument out of the blue and now she wanted straight talk. All right – she'd get straight talk.

'I didn't mention your father,' he reminded her steadily, 'but, if you want me to illustrate my particular story, a rancher like your father – a Mister Big who was hogging all the range around my home – put me on the owl-hoot trail. He made me see that the little fellow has to make his stand with a gun in his fist. You can't be a Gentle Annie in the West; my father was a gentle man – and the big fellow put him into his grave!'

The girl's mouth was pressed into a straight and hard line as she glared at the marshal of Santa Rita.

'You can't sit under my father's roof and insult him,' she declared. 'If it wasn't for him, you wouldn't be marshal of the town. He recommended you be sent for after one of the hands said he knew you were up north! You can't accept Rafter R hospitality and insult my father!'

'Look,' Barradell began firmly, 'I don't owe your father for anything except the rest I'm takin' on his property right now an' the dressin' of my wound, which I rightly owe to you. Dressin' the injuries of the ailin' is only what the Testament tells you to do, so that won't come hard to a virtuous person like yoreself that don't like gunfighters,' he added archly.

The girl snorted.

'When it comes to yore father sendin' for me, he did so because he wanted this territory riddin' of the Border Bunch, so he can run more cattle an' make more money. I don't figure I owe him much!' In his mind, Barradell added: 'If I owe anyone anythin' I owe bullets to Al Poindexter's bushwhackers.' Al Poindexter, trying to live down his bullet-bitten past by throwing his guns into the service of the law, was growing as a symbol in Barradell's mind. He and Poindexter, the two-gun trigger-slick men others were quick to condemn, were of the same breed – but Poindexter had been shot in the back before he really had a chance to set himself square with his law-guns.

The rustle of a skirt sounded from the door of the living-room and a cold voice said: 'I seem to hear strong words.'

Alicia Riddle, fresh-faced and wearing riding costume, came into the room, halting at the doorway when she saw Barradell.

The marshal stood up and nodded a 'good-morning' to the girl.

Charlie Riddle's second daughter seemed to forget the argument with Barradell as her sister appeared.

'Alicia, have you been out riding – with *him*?' she enquired. Her tone seemed almost shocked.

'And if I have,' sniffed the classic-featured Alicia, 'what is that to you, Jenny?'

'You know what father's opinion of him is,' her sister retorted.

Barradell was thinking: 'Jenny, so that's the little spitfire's name.' He wondered who the mysterious *him* was, but the answer was supplied by the memory of the previous night in Mannix's store and the expression that had come to Alicia Riddle's face at the mention of Doctor George Merriam's name.

'I don't care what father's opinion is,' Alicia declared frigidly.

Barradell's mind was suddenly elsewhere.

In a corner of the room, directly opposite from where he sat, was a small table on which stood a tall bottle of a good brand of whiskey and an empty glass. On the floor close to the table was a small heap of that peculiar red sand.

Someone with red sand on his, or her boots had

recently stood close to the table, possibly in order to pour a drink. The marshal reflected that it would hardly be Riddle's daughter, Jenny, and a quick glance at her dainty shoes peeking from below the sweeping blue gown showed them to be free of traces of sand. Maybe that sand was located elsewhere than on that section of the desert where he came across the hurriedly riding Claffin, but he had so far seen that particular redness in the sand of that single location.

Thought of Claffin caused him to wonder whether the Texas cow-thief had yet recovered. He made a move for the door.

'Thanks for the medical attention,' he told Jenny Riddle. 'I'm beholden to you.'

'It was nothing,' the girl replied coldly. 'Nothing to virtuous people like myself who don't like gunfighters!'

Barradell replied with a hard grin quirking his features:

'Touché, Miss Riddle!'

They held a brief pose, a triangle of people standing quite still in strained silence – tough, gun-packing Barradell; the haughty, classic-featured Alicia and her younger, more likeable spitfire of a sister.

Then the pose was broken by the double blast of a six-gun from somewhere out on the yard of the Rafter R.

SIX

Barradell ran headlong from the room, across the gallery and down the steps, clawing his Colt from leather as he went. A flat drift of gun-smoke was hazing up from the back of the long structure of the bunkhouse and the sudden thunder of a horse's hooves began from the back of the building.

The marshal of Santa Rita came off the steps with a powerful spring and slithered across the dust of the yard. The yard was completely empty until a piebald horse, with a dark-garbed man in its saddle, came lunging out from the back of the bunkhouse. Its rider was crouching low, so that Barradell could not see his face, he held a naked six-shooter in one hand and he urged his steed for the far fence of the yard with rapidly spurring heels.

The black-garbed rider turned his head almost the instant Barradell came off the gallery steps and the Marshal had a brief glimpse of a square of black cloth entirely covering the face under the wide black sombrero.

The mystery rider's hand came up in a quick arc, as he made for the fence, the sun putting a dull blue sheen on the metal of his gun. Barradell twisted himself to one side as the other's six-gun slammed out in a blossom of flame. The slug whanged across the yard like an angry hornet and bit a chunk of adobe out of the ranch-house gallery with a puff of white dust. Then, the hurtling rider was taking the peeled-pole fence. Barradell fired a split-second too late and the bullet from his gun screamed within an inch of the rider's hat as he went down the other side of the fence to the wide rangeland beyond.

The marshal looked hastily around the yard. There was not a horse in sight; someone had led his own gelding away, probably to feed and water it.

All right, he couldn't give chase to the mystery masked rider who had tried to kill him the moment he first saw him, but the man was forking his horse, splitting the wind out there on the open rangeland and still within pistol range. Barradell positioned himself to peg another shot after the fleeing rider.

He was interrupted by a hoarse croak from the direction of the bunkhouse, turned his head and saw Charlie Riddle staggering out of the long, low structure of the Rafter R riders' quarters.

'Barradell! Give me a hand here!' the rancher said urgently.

The gunfighter turned his head again in the direction of the fence. The madly-hurtling rider in black was dwindling now and well out of six-gun range.

'Blast him!' cursed Barradell. 'He's got plumb away!'

He moved towards the bunkhouse. Riddle was trembling and white-faced.

'Come in here, Barradell,' urged the rancher. Barradell thought bleakly that the owner of the Rafter R had used his correct name twice while it had been decided by the law and order bunch of Santa Rita that he would conceal his identity under the name of Smith. It was a farce and folly, thought the gunfighter, a leopard couldn't change his spots and a triggerslick couldn't change his name and shed his reputation for long. He followed Riddle into the bunkhouse. The bunk-lined building was heavy with the acrid stench of cordite smoke, a window was shattered and close to it lay Bull Claffin, sprawled on a bunk with a red-welling hole in his chest.

Ed, the cowhand who helped the rancher tote the unconscious man into the bunkhouse, was slumped facedown on the floor. A creeping crimson trickle inched from under his body and across the scuffed boards of the floor. Once glance told Barradell that both the Texas rustler and the cowhand were dead.

'What happened?' he demanded of Riddle.

'Claffin was just coming round when we heard the sound of a horse in the yard. Suddenly, I saw a face at the window – at least, I saw a hat and a mask – then whoever was outside fired through the glass and hit Claffin full in the chest. Ed went for his gun and the man outside fired again. Ed went down before he had his gun clear of leather. I ducked for cover, I'm not wearing a gun, and the man outside fired at me. He missed and made off!'

An urgent needle of caution stabbed at Barradell. He thought:

He's lying! There were only two shots! Two and no more.

On the heels of the thought came wonderment as to why Bull Claffin should have been murdered so dramatically and the answer suggested itself. Because he might talk about the Border Bunch. Because he could not be trusted to keep his mouth tight closed when Barradell got around to asking about the identity of the leader of the renegades and the whereabouts of the gang's hiding-hole. Someone – a tall rider, dressed in black – had followed the marshal and his prisoner to the Rafter R and killed the big Texan to ensure his silence. Or had he followed them? Maybe the killer was at the ranch the whole time.

Barradell stood regarding the two corpses with bitter feelings. He suddenly remembered that little heap of red sand close to the table in the ranch-house and looked instinctively to the boots of Charlie Riddle.

Caked in the ridge of the welt of his tooled leather riding-boots, not in great quantity, but enough for the marshal to make no mistake, was a line of red sand. That same red sand he'd seen on the floor of the law-officer's quarters back in Santa Rita, the same red sand that seemed peculiar to that section of desert near the red sandstone wall where he located Bull Claffin.

The marshal of Santa Rita glowered at Riddle. The hatred of all grasping ranchers that had grown with him suddenly surged up inside him. Riddle of the

Rafter R was in with the Border Bunch, he was sure. The chairman of Santa Rita's Law and Order Committee was running with the hounds and thinking with the hare – but was he the big man? This killing of Claffin and the Rafter R puncher on Riddle's ranch was no surprise to Riddle, although he was acting the part of a shocked man extremely well. Something had gone on in this bunkhouse when the masked man appeared and doubtless Ed, the cowhand, was put out of the way because he saw or heard something, and that meant he, at least, was not tied up with the Border Bunch. Barradell kept his temper and thought of the rest of Riddle's crew. With an outfit the size of the Rafter R there'd have to be a large bunch of riders – were they the rank and file of the rampaging Border Bunch?

'Where are the rest of yore men?' he asked calmly.

'Out on my east pasture, miles from here. There's a heap of work to be done over there and the whole crew is engaged on it. Ed here was the only one who didn't go out.'

'That was hard on Ed,' commented Barradell flatly. 'An' it was powerful convenient for the guy who killed Claffin an' Ed that the place was deserted an' that my geldin' was tied up somewhere where I couldn't get at him to chase that *hombre*.'

Riddle's eyes flared a little. It was evident that he did not miss the implied suspicion of himself in the words.

'Yes,' he murmured. 'And I've lost a good rider in Ed and you've lost a prisoner.'

'A mighty handy prisoner;' added the lawman, 'who would have told me plenty once I got to persuadin' him. Seems like the Border Bunch realized that, too.'

He turned and moved for the door, walking into the sun-washed yard.

'Where's my cayuse?' he demanded, without turning his head.

'In the barn,' answered Charlie Riddle. 'I put him in there to rest and feed.'

'I'll see you some more,' Barradell called by way of a farewell.

And, to Riddle, it sounded like a threat.

There was a rider about half a mile ahead of Barradell when he reached the heat-hazed flat across which lay Santa Rita. A black-clad rider in a big-brimmed sombrero in whose wake hazed a drift of sun-touched dust. The marshal spurred up his gelding, came close to the rider headed up trail before him and called:

'Hey there, *hombre*! Hold yore horse!'

The cut of the other man's black coat, the black sombrero and his general build reminded him of the rider who shot Claffin and the Rafter R puncher at Riddle's ranch, although the mystery man rode a piebald and the one in front of him rode a chestnut.

At the sound of the marshal's voice, the black-clad rider turned his head and Barradell saw the neatly-trimmed beard and moustache of Dr George Merriam. Barradell spurred his horse up towards the other rider, wondering whether the gunslinging medico could have been the masked killer at the Rafter R. To his mind came the memory of Alicia Riddle's conversation with her sister. She admitted she had been riding with a man her father disliked and there was little doubt in the lawman's mind that her riding-companion was Merriam, which meant Merriam had been somewhere in the vicinity of the Rafter R – but was he the man who fired the two shots through the bunkhouse window?

Merriam offered him a tough grin as he drew alongside him. Barradell came to the point at once.

'Merriam, have you been anywhere on Rafter R property?' he demanded. He considered the doctor's size and build as he spoke. In his black broadcloth, he could have been the man who had exchanged shots with him in the yard of Riddle's ranch, but there was the business of the horse. If Merriam was indeed the slayer of Claffin and the Rafter R cowboy, how did he contrive to change the piebald for a chestnut?

The gun-throwing medico's answer came calmly; obviously, this was one time when he was stone cold sober.

'I have – as near as I dare go to the Rafter R, Marshal Smith. The owner of that outfit doesn't care for me, so I keep away from his headquarters.'

Barradell eyed him narrowly.

'Would that be far enough away for you to know nothing about a double killin' at the Rafter R?' he queried.

What appeared to be genuine surprise showed in the eyes of the wayward doctor.

'I don't know what you're talking about, marshal,' he countered.

'Listen, Merriam, you're the damnedest puzzle I ever came across in this place of puzzles. I'm not mixin' my words. A man who was my prisoner an' one of Riddle's hands were shot dead less than an hour ago. I saw the man who shot them. He looked mighty like you in build, but he was masked – an' you're ridin' from the direction of the Rafter R. Were you the man who shot those two?'

'So that was what I heard,' mused the doctor, rubbing his bearded chin. 'I heard a couple of shots just as I was striking back for town. I wasn't the man who did the killing at the Rafter R, marshal, tell me more about it.'

'When you tell me more,' Barradell said sharply. 'I don't understand you, Merriam. I don't know who you're runnin' with, or thinkin' with. You threw yore guns into my fight against Albertson an' those Border Bunch hangers-on, but there's quite a deal of double-dealin' goin' on around here. I don't know who stands where! I want to know how near you were to the Rafter R when you heard those shots an' if you saw anyone hazin' away from the ranch.'

The bearded young man riding beside him turned to face the marshal squarely. There was that in his face which instinctively made Barradell want to trust him.

'Let's set ourselves square, marshal. I was about five miles on this side of the Rafter R when I heard those shots and I didn't see anyone riding away from there.'

Barradell thought quickly: 'That means the masked

rider must have travelled southward – in the direction of that tract of red sand and the red wall of rock in the desert.' Whichever way the business was looked at, that red wall and that tract of sand – sand which Al Poindexter had once investigated, sand which found its way to the boots of double-dealing Charlie Riddle – always turned up in the end.

'If you think I'm in with the Border Bunch, you're wrong, marshal,' continued Merriam. 'I was on Rafter R land because I was riding with Riddle's elder daughter – you might as well know she's all I give a damn for in the whole world, but Riddle hates my insides. I left Alicia a short distance from the ranch and then headed back for town, riding slowly.'

Jeff Barradell grunted. Instinctively, he trusted this wild, lead-throwing young medical man and he wondered again what the reckless Merriam was trying to put at his back with his devil-may-care border-town mode of life. He recollected Doc Holliday, lately of Tombstone, now languishing in Colorado with an Arizona warrant over his head. With Doc, the cultured Georgia dentist, it was the certainty that he would never recover from consumption that drove him to gunslinging without the smallest care for his skin. There was something of that same eagerness to seek trouble in George Merriam – he had demonstrated it that night when Albertson hoorawed Santa Rita – but it was obviously not brought about by sickness.

Barradell spat into the dust of the trail. Whatever prodded the doctor into his wild life was his business and no one else's, he thought. It was something bitter, he supposed, like his own owl-hoot days, like the story of his turning in a partner to gain a free pardon – bitter with that same bitterness that lay in the back-trail of poor Al Poindexter, his bushwhacked predecessor.

He glanced at the bearded man riding at his shoulder. Merriam was cynical-featured and yet there was some compelling genuine quality about him.

The adobe structures of Santa Rita loomed larger before them.

SEVEN

Barradell parted with Merriam at the small hotel on Santa Rita's main street where the doctor lived. Thinking of the happenings of that morning, he rode steadily on to the jail, took his gelding into the stable behind it and entered the cramped living quarters.

Sitting on the bed, he dwelt on the major discovery of his ride out of town. Charlie Riddle was running with the Border Bunch. He was sure of it – the sand on the rancher's shoes, the lie about the mystery man shooting three shots instead of two to cover the fact that, of the trio in the bunkhouse, Riddle alone remained alive – these facts pointed to it. The memory of the sand – that same red sand – he found on the floor of this very apartment came to mind. Somewhere in the region of that tract of red desert sand lay the Border Bunch's hide-out; anyone who went there could scarcely avoid collecting it on his boots. Al Poindexter had been investigating in that vicinity and the Border Bunch had bushwhacked him. To Jeff Barradell, it was as plain as day.

Another fact needled at his consciousness. If Riddle was in with the rampaging border renegades, what of the other members of the Law and Order Committee? Mannix seemed genuine enough, but there were other members; were they, too, running with the hounds and thinking with the hare, in the fashion of the organization's chairman?

The big question of the morning's investigation stared the marshal of Santa Rita in the face. Was Charlie Riddle the big boss of the Border Bunch? Or was he a pawn of someone else?

And why was Bull Claffin killed? What urgent information had he that the Border Bunch should send a blackclad killer out of nowhere to silence him with a bullet rather than risk his breaking down and talking to the marshal under duress?

Barradell flexed the muscle of the arm which Bull Claffin's bullet had nicked. Bull was a stupid oaf, more often the tool of other lawbreakers than a rogue himself – strangely, although he had himself threatened to shoot Bull, Barradell was sorry the big Texas cow-thief had fallen victim to the Border Bunch in that mysterious business at the Rafter R. Well, that was just another score to settle with the renegades. He'd sling a few slugs on Bull's behalf and for Ed, too, as well as the bushwhacked Al Poindexter, when the lead began to fly in earnest.

Meantime, he'd stay in town and watch and wait.

Later, he crossed the street and ate a meal in a gloomy little eating-house, operated by a buxom Mexican woman, then he ambled along the street to

the cantina where he'd made his play against blustering Dutch Albertson the previous night. He had two
drinks – from the good bottle – then walked over the
rutted and hoof-pocked dust of the street to Mannix's
store. Throughout his progression around the town,
walking to the eating-house, to the cantina and over to
the general store, he was aware of the populace watching him. He knew what was going on in heads behind
those shrewd eyes. They were thinking: *There he goes,
another of the owl-hoot breed, trying to build himself
some self-respect by playing lawman – now he's bought
the law off his own tail by selling out a partner!*

Or they were thinking: *Here comes the new marshal
– another walking target for the Border Bunch!*

Let them think what they liked. Maybe they didn't
like him, but they had to fall back on his kind when
they wanted their town taming. The smart-alecky
reformers, with their high ideals and windy talk, just
didn't have the guts to do the job the only way it could
be done – with bullets.

Three or four women, Americans, were fussing
around what appeared to be a newly-arrived consignment of dress material when Barradell entered
Mannix's store. A couple of leathery-faced, pioneer-
looking men were leaning against the counter, smoking, and the hunched-up figure of the Papago, still
sleeping, seemed not to have shifted since the marshal
first saw it the evening before.

Both weatherbeaten pioneers offered him a taci-
turn nod, their heads bobbing as if activated by the
same spring. Barradell nodded back and waited until

Mannix had served the women and they went out of the store in a swish of trailing skirts. The store was empty now, save for its owner, Barradell and the leathery-faced oldsters.

Mannix came out from behind his counter and introduced the pair to the marshal.

'Marshal Smith, these here are Tom Skinner an' Carl Wills, two of our Law an' Order Committee. The three exchanged nods again and grunted 'how d'you dos'. Barradell, thinking of the chairman of the citizen's law group and the deep suspicion he had of him scrutinized the two older men. He didn't see treachery in those grim, honest-as-the-earth faces. Nevertheless, a man couldn't know who was what in this town, so Barradell decided to hold his tongue with regard to the strong suspicion he had of Riddle and the shooting of the rustler and cowhand at the Rafter R.

Barradell purchased a sack of tobacco and papers from the storekeeper and proceeded to roll a smoke.

'How're you likin' Santa Rita, marshal?' asked Tom Skinner.

'It's lively enough for me,' Barradell grunted.

Over by the open door, the blanketed Papago Indian suddenly started, his attention taken by something out on the street. His dark gaze was fixed on something out there, unseen by the men in the stores. From under the blanket came a stream of Indian dialect intermingled with which Barradell heard the Spanish words *mal hombre*.

'Bad man?' he questioned, moving towards the door. 'Where?'

He stood close to the huddled Indian, scanning the dusty, sun-washed ribbon of the street. A man was riding a big grey full in the centre of the street, coming at a slow, determined walk. He was a slim man, dressed in the garb of the range. A wide-brimmed Stetson was cuffed back on his head to make a dusty halo around the back of his square features. From under the hat, straggles of lank blond hair flopped over his broad brow. Two six-guns were belted at his thighs and he sat his saddle with a slight forward tilt to his upper body. Slowly, the big grey horse came up the street, side-stepping over the sun-touched dust occasionally with the fractiousness of an animal sensing trouble.

The rider came steadily onward. He rode with his features set into a stolid mask and serape-wrapped Mexicans, American women and their lean, dusty-jeaned men moved out of his way as he progressed up the middle of the street, dominating the town by his presence.

Mannix came to Barradell's shoulder, contemplated the newcomer with wide eyes and exclaimed:

'Larsen – Swede Larsen – he's one of the Border Bunch!'

'Swede Larsen, out of Utah!' grunted Barradell. 'I've heard of him!' He ducked back behind the door.

'He's lookin' for me, I don't doubt. Where's yore back door?'

Mannix nodded in the direction of his living-room.

'Straight through there – it leads to the alley.'

Barradell moved for the rear room quickly. As he

went, he heard the oldster, Carl Wills, watching the street around the edge of the door, declare:

'He's headed right across for the jail!'

The marshal of Santa Rita hastened through the small room at the back of the store and into the alleyway with its scatterings of trash and rusted cans. He moved swiftly along, heading for an opening between the store and the harness-maker's shop which would bring him out on the street almost opposite the jail. He rounded the back of the store and crouched into the shadows of the smaller cross-alley. He saw the width of the dusty street and, across it, the alley running to the rear of the jail. The back of the big grey, with its gun-heavy rider, was moving down that alley and in the very act of turning around into the open area at the back where was located the stable and the door to Barradell's quarters.

'Payin' me a call, is he?' mused the marshal. 'All right, I'll go across an' greet him.'

He moved down the small alley with quick strides, emerged on the street and paced directly across its width to the alley at the side of the *caliboza*. As he walked, his right hand hung limp at his side, the palm pushing the butt of the Colt in the tied-down holster. On the plank-walks, apprehensive citizens stood under the warped store-awnings, watching him move quickly across the street from alley to alley.

Ten minutes before, Doctor George Merriam had been standing on the wooden-railed second-storey gallery of the Southwest House, the hotel in which he lived. He saw the tall gunslinger with his grimly

determined air come pacing his big grey along the
street and held a stiff pose, watching Swede Larsen
fixedly.

He saw the Utah gunman wheel his horse around
the side of the jail.

'Going for Barradell, eh?' he commented to himself.
'Seems like I should be in on this.'

He whipped back the skirt of his frock-coat with a
decisive action, revealing the Smith & Wesson
holstered at his slug-studded belt, turned on his heel
and strode quickly off the gallery.

Cautiously, he emerged on to the street from the
main entrance of the Southwest House just in time to
see the marshal go striding determinedly across from
the alley between the harness-maker's and Mannix's
store, then disappear along into the mouth of the alley
into which the mounted Larsen had turned.

Unhurriedly, Merriam strolled along the plank-
walk in the direction of the jail.

Jeff Barradell, treading like a man walking on glass
eggs so that his spurs did not ring, edged along the
alley. Just before he rounded the rear of the jail building, he drew his six-shooter from its leather.

The open tract of land at the back of the jail was
empty, save for Swede Larsen's big grey tethered to a
peeled-pole rail close to the small lean-to stable.

Barradell scanned the dusty area quickly. There
was no sign of the blond gunman. The opening of the
lean-to stable was dark, but the marshal could see his
gelding inside, standing quietly, its quietness indicat-
ing that Larsen was not hiding in there.

So he was in the living quarters at the back of the jail, probably waiting with a ready gun for Barradell to come through the door.

The marshal considered the grey tethered outside the stable. The presence of the horse was a jarring note. If Swede Larsen came here to lie up for him in the living-room at the rear of the *caliboza*, why did he advertise his presence by leaving his mount outside. Indeed, if he came to Santa Rita to kill Barradell, why did he ride so boldly along the street?

Barradell inched towards the door of his quarters, gun prodding and trigger-finger tensed.

'Are you in there, Larsen?' he called.

A hard, gritty-edged voice answered from the room beyond the warped wooden door which stood ajar:

'Yeah, I'm in here, marshal, waitin' for you to come in – I want to make talk with you.'

Barradell stepped towards the door with a final, long stride, touched the sun-split wood with his boot-heel and sent the door creaking open, his gun was levelled in readiness to meet lead with lead and his body was taut, keyed to spring to one side if Swede Larsen was positioned square in front of the door to gun him down as he entered.

No gun-song clattered from the room and there was no sign of the lean, blond gunman of the Border Bunch. The marshal of Santa Rita moved through the portal and, as if timed to the precise instant, a grown, sinewy hand came around the open door and clapped the hard, round mouth of a six-shooter to his temple.

'Drop yore hardware!' ordered the voice of Swede

Larsen from where he stood pressed against the back of the open door. 'I've got the drop on you, marshal, an' you know it. Drop yore iron an' we can talk peaceable like, but with me holdin' the gun!'

Inwardly, Jeff Barradell cursed and thought: 'I walked into it like a wet-behind-the ears kid!'

He knew the other had the drop on him with that gun pressed against his head.

So he dropped his Colt.

EIGHT

Swede Larsen chuckled. It was a dry and humourless chuckle and the hand snaked around the edge of the door pressed the gun closer to Barradell's head.

'Come right in, marshal,' invited the Utah gunman, 'an' don't attempt any smart-alecky moves!'

Barradell stepped over his dropped revolver into the small room. Larsen moved with him, coming out from his hiding-place. The blond gunslinger kicked the door with his heel as he moved and the door creaked shut with a note of finality. Larsen moved his gun from the marshal's head and covered him square on the belt-buckle. He jerked his square, Stetson-haloed head towards the bunk.

'Sit over there, Mister Barradell!' He said the name with a calculated deliberation.

Jeff Barradell moved over to the bunk and sat on it, facing the Border Bunch gunman and wondering what he was here for.

Swede Larsen seated himself on the edge of the rough table, keeping his hard blue eyes and his gun levelled on the marshal of Santa Rita. Working by touch, he located his sack of makings in his shirt-pocket with his left hand. He tossed the sack to Barradell.

'Roll me a smoke, marshal, an' one for yourself,' he ordered. 'You an' me are goin' to have a talk; ain't no reason why we shouldn't smoke over it.'

Barradell knew the order to roll a smoke for the blond gunman was a studied insult. He opened the sack of Bull Durham and rolled two cigarettes under the gun and the cold smile of Swede Larsen.

He tossed one to the gunman but there was no catching him off balance to make him take his eyes from the man he covered. He caught the smoke adroitly, fixed it into his hard smile, produced a match which he lit with a flick of a hard thumb-nail and applied to the cigarette. He leaned slightly forward and lit Barradell's.

'I'll lay it square on the line, Barradell,' he stated flatly. 'The Border Bunch can use you – there's a place for a man with a quick gun.'

Barradell started. This was something quite unexpected. He faced Swede Larsen's hard smile with bleak eyes.

'This some kind of joke, Larsen?' he queried.

'No joke. The Border Bunch can use you.'

'The big man sent you to tell me that, eh?'

'Yeah, he sent me to tell you. Smart guy, the big boss, he's got plenty of savvy an' he knows all about men with big gun-reputations.'

Barradell quirked his lips into a tough smile.

'Didn't anybody ever tell him I've reformed?' he asked.

Swede Larsen matched the tough smile with his own cold grin. The note of humour that had been lacking in his smile crept to his blue eyes.

'Oh, sure,' he smirked loftily. 'Changed yore spots like a leopard can. Turned yore gun-partner in for a state's pardon. Sure, the boss heard about that. And he believes you've reformed — like hell!'

'What happens if I don't feel any inclination to throw in with you?' Barradell wanted to know.

'An easy question to answer,' smiled Larsen. 'I kill you.'

Barradell felt a surge of coldness rise in him. He knew that Swede Larsen was a six-gun killer with a big reputation. He wondered if the Border Bunch made this same proposition to Al Poindexter before he found his bushwhack grave. Maybe they had. They'd make it in much the same way: 'You sold out yore partner, Poindexter, but you're as much a gunnie as you ever were an' the Border Bunch can use you.'

And Poindexter had bucked them — defied them until they gunned him out of his saddle from a desert ambush. The symbol of Poindexter seemed to grow larger to Jeff Barradell. His reputation was spotty, but he'd turned to the law and upheld his law-officer's position until he was murdered.

Barradell blew out a thin streamer of smoke.

'Did yore outlaw crowd make this kind of offer to Poindexter?' he asked calmly, although his heart was pounding like a trip-hammer.

Over by the door, he could see his Colt lying on the floor. The door, swinging shut under Larsen's kick, had swiped the gun and sent it slithering over the boards to lie in a corner at the foot of the bunk on which Barradell was seated. If only he could make a grab for it, he thought with a panicky edge goading him.

At the mention of Poindexter's name, Larsen's grim smile widened. A hard, rattling chuckle sounded from somewhere in his throat.

'Poindexter!' he grunted. 'You should ask about Poindexter!'

Barradell's eyes darted to the gun on the floor, then back to the square face of the gunman on the table. Maybe, he thought wildly, he could lurch off the bunk to sprawl on the floor and grab the Colt. It would be mighty dangerous to try that move under the outlaw's gun and the chances of success were almost negligible.

'Well?' asked Larsen, pulling at his cigarette and allowing dribbles of smoke to issue from his mouth with his words. 'How do you feel about it, Mister Fast-gun Barradell? They say you built yoreself a tolerable big reputation in Nevada an' Wyomin' an' other places. You turned in yore partner, but the big boss won't hold that against you, I guess.' This seemed to afford him amusement for some reason and he chuckled his rasping chuckle again. 'I guess,' he concluded at length, 'it's high time you dropped this phoney Smith game, Barradell an' came out in yore real colours.'

Barradell drew on his shortening ricepaper cigarette, drew it from his mouth and studied its glowing end.

He looked at Larsen's smirking face again. Smoke was trickling from the gunslinger's lips, swirling up past his flat, broad cheekbones and causing him to half close his eyes.

It was seeing Larsen's eyes half closed in this manner that spurred Barradell into quick action. With a speedy sweep of his arm, he pitched the cigarette full into the blond gunman's face.

Larsen squawked as the red end of the smoke caught him in his eye and Barradell was sending his body hurtling off the end of the bunk to hit the floor and claw for the Colt.

Even as he smote the rough boarding of the floor with the palms of his hands, Barradell knew he'd pulled a fool move. The six-gun was inches from his fingertips and Larsen had recovered from the unexpected stab of the lighted cigarette against his eye. He was standing now, with his gun levelled at the man on the floor. And he was chuckling.

'Grab for it, Barradell,' he hissed out of his smiling lips. 'Grab for it an' I'll gun you full of holes.'

The tall, blond gunman held his position, spread-legged – waiting and smirking. From the floor, Jeff Barradell could see the killer's intention written on his face.

'The big boss was wrong about you, Barradell,' he purred. 'You did change yore spots – you really are a lawman through an' through. Now, grab that gun – so I can say I riddled the great Jeff Barradell while he had a gun in his hand!'

He motioned impatiently with his six-gun.

'Grab it!' he snarled. 'I said—'

Barradell heard the bellowing blast of a gun filling the small room. Distantly, he was aware of the tinkle of shattering glass; then he saw Larsen teetering forward as if hinged in the middle. He hit the floor face on, heaving a sobbing sigh as he went. He lay still, inches from where Barradell sprawled.

A jagged-edged star was shattered in the sand-crusted window pane.

Cordite smoke hazed in the room. Beyond the curtain of swirling, acrid musk, the door was kicked open and the frock-coated form of George Merriam strode in with his Smith & Wesson smoking in his hand.

'I had to give it to him in the back,' he commented matter-of-factly. 'He was fixing to kill you.'

Barradell came up off the floor half dazed. The tableau before him – the broken window, the man sprawled in death, brought an echo of the double shooting at the Rafter R earlier that day and awoke the suspicion that Merriam was the man who fired through the window of the bunkhouse.

The youthful doctor holstered his pistol.

'I saw Larsen riding into town,' he said. 'I knew he was looking for trouble as soon as I saw him. When I saw him come around here, I followed. When I heard voices coming from behind the door, I took a peek through the window and saw him with his gun levelled on you. I waited awhile then I saw you make that move for the gun. When it was evident he had you to rights and intended killing you, I let him have it.'

Barradell cuffed dust from his clothing.

'I'm obliged to you, Merriam, that's the second time you poked yore gun in on my account.' he replied. 'Did you hear the proposition he made me?'

'I heard it. The Big Boss of the Border Bunch wanted you to join up with his outfit. They figured you haven't changed your spots.'

'I've changed my spots, all right, Merriam,' the marshal stated grimly, 'and, while we're both together in private, where do you stand in regard to the Border Bunch?'

'I don't stand with them, if that's what's eating you, marshal,' Merriam answered with vehemence. 'If I did, would I go shooting up Butch Albertson's hangers-on, or this fellow here?'

'And yet you don't stand with the Law and Order Committee!'

'Law and Order Committee!' repeated Merriam with scorn. 'They don't want me, I want them less. You must know their kind – well-intentioned but weak. They can't do much of their own accord, they have to send for a reputation gunhand to enforce their law – no offence intended to you, but you know the way of it. These storekeepers and small businessmen are the first to despise a man who lives by his gun but, when they need a gun on their side of the gamble, they damn soon forget their petty respectability.'

Jeff Barradell nodded agreement. He was all too aware of the truth of the bearded doctor's words. Petty respectability was stacked against the man forced to the night-trails once he tried to cast off his owl-hoot ways, but the same virtuous folk who despised him would not hesitate in buying his gunskill when smoke-talk was required to preserve their comfort. The marshal of Santa Rita found himself liking this enigmatic, gunslinging medico with his habit of showing up when he was most needed.

Barradell fished in his shirt-pocket, produced his makings and began to roll a cigarette. He reflected on the doctor's scorn of the Law and Order Committee and wondered what his opinion of its chairman was.

'Merriam,' he ventured, 'who do you think is the boss of the Border Bunch?'

George Merriam smiled under his long-sweeping moustache.

'Could be anybody,' he said unhelpfully.

'Anybody like Charlie Riddle, for instance?' suggested the lawman.

Merriam considered that in silence while each regarded the other as Barradell lit his smoke.

'Charlie Riddle's had cattle run off by the Border Bunch,' the medico pointed out, 'but that doesn't mean a thing in the long-run. I don't like Riddle, but I don't think he's the boss of the Border Bunch, which isn't to say he might not be running with them. He's the grasping kind, marshal; you know, the same old cattle dream – he sees himself as the lord of a big cow-empire hereabouts.'

'Yeah, I know his kind,' Barradell declared. 'His kind killed my father back in Nevada. I had Riddle spotted for a money man when I first saw him.'

'What makes you suspicious of him?' Merriam asked.

'Two or three things,' the marshal said evasively. 'I'm not sure he wasn't in on the killing of Bull Claffin an' that Rafter R hand. I guess I should never have allowed Claffin out of my sight; he was shot because he might talk if I persuaded him hard enough, I'm nearly sure of that. The ranch hand was shot because he must have realized that his boss – possibly because of some action or word on Riddle's part – was in cahoots with the man at the window and Riddle told me a lie about the man at the window takin' a shot at him when there were only two shots.'

'Hmm,' mused Merriam, tugging thoughtfully at his beard. 'I don't like Riddle and he doesn't like me, mainly because I've fallen head over heels for his daughter. Can't say I ever thought of him as the big man of the Border Bunch, though.' He changed the subject suddenly. 'You know what you need – a deputy, and I'm the man for the job!'

Barradell started.

'A deputy – you?'

'Sure. I'm supposed to be worthless, but I can use a gun and you and I are basically two of a kind. Will you swear me in?'

Barradell remembered the way the tempestuous, leadthrowing doctor aided him in the fight with Butch Albertson and, contemplating the stiffening form of Swede Larsen, reflected on how he had saved him from certain death only a few minutes before.

'Maybe it's a matter for the Law an' Order Committee who's sworn in or not,' he observed. Then, the folly of such a thought struck him. If the Law and

Order Committee had the say in who were to serve as peace officers and the committee was ramrodded by a Border Bunch man, then there would never be an end to corruption around Santa Rita. 'Wait a minute,' he added. 'A peace officer can elect who he thinks fit as deputies once he's been sworn in. I'm sworn in an' I can swear you in, too.'

Merriam promptly raised his right hand and Barradell performed the ceremony. He went into the office fronting the jail and produced a deputy's star from the drawer, took it back to the living-quarters and handed it to Merriam.

'Now,' he said, with a nod at the sprawled form of Swede Larsen, 'let's make arrangements to have him planted on cemetery hill.'

NINE

Jeff Barradell spent a night of fitful sleep on his bunk in the room behind the *caliboza*.

All night, thoughts of the mysterious double killing at the Rafter R, of Merriam's timely intervention when Swede Larsen was about to squeeze his trigger, of Riddle, Claffin, Poindexter, who was a haunting symbol to him now, a bushwhacked lawman of his own kind, crying out for vengeance, passed through his mind. For some reason, Butch Albertson troubled his dreams.

He awoke with Albertson still on his mind and found himself thinking of the big, blustering Texan as he prepared his breakfast of canned beans, pork and coffee.

It dawned on him that of the Border Bunch crew of renegades, with the exception of Riddle on whom he had strong suspicions, Albertson was the only one whose stamping-ground he knew. He recalled that Albertson, on the night of the gunfight at the cantina, told him he had a cabin on a water-hole at

Conquistadore Rim, wherever that was. If anyone could be persuaded to talk of where the Border Bunch hung out, who was their leader and why Bull Claffin had been shot at the Rafter R, it must surely be Albertson who was craven, despite his size and bluster.

'Maybe,' he told the blackened coffee-pot as he poured himself a cupful of its contents, 'I'll take a pasear over towards Conquistadore Rim this morning.'

Following breakfast, he ambled along the street of Santa Rita where life was beginning to stir. He moved casually along to the Southwest House, entered the hotel and found Merriam in the ground-floor dining-room beginning breakfast.

Merriam. nodded to a chair and indicated a tall bottle of good whiskey which Barradell declined because of the earliness of the day. Merriam seemed to prefer whiskey where others took coffee.

'You busy this mornin'?' inquired the marshal.

'No. Not even another Mexican baby to deliver, so far as I know, why?'

'How does a man get to Conquistadore Rim?'

'It's a fair ride out of town. What makes you want to go over in that direction?'

'Albertson hangs out there. He might answer a few questions if we talk to him.'

Merriam sank the last of a glassful of whiskey and wiped his mouth with a napkin.

'I'll come with you.' he stated. 'You'll need someone to show you the way and you might need some help with that big Texas ape.'

Barradell waited until the doctor finished his meal

and they strode out of the Southwest House together. Almost as soon as they stepped on to the plank-walk they encountered Charlie Riddle and his daughters stepping down from a buckboard and obviously just arrived in town on a shopping expedition.

Both tipped their hats to the young women, Merriam bringing a softening to the haughty features of Alicia while Jenny merely sniffed and turned her head away with a lofty air as Barradell paid his compliments. Doubtless, the girl remembered the previous day's verbal wrangle with the lean gunslinger, but her aversion to him was not so acute as she affected and she bestowed a furtive and quite unhostile glance upon him when she thought he was not looking. Barradell did not miss it.

Something was on the rancher's mind and his approach to Barradell and Merriam was distinctly unfriendly.

'What's this about you becoming deputy marshal, Merriam?' he demanded. 'Is it true?'

'It's true,' the medico told him coldly.

'Your business is medicine, Merriam,' the rancher snapped. 'This town expects you to be its doctor, not a lawman.'

'Don't tell me my business, Riddle,' Merriam answered levelly and completely without emotion. 'This town needn't presume to expect anything of me – it'll get from me what I choose to give it.'

Riddle was flushing, sharp anger flaring his nostrils and bringing a glow to his eyes. He turned to his daughters.

'Move along and start your purchasing, girls,' he told them in an ill-controlled voice. 'I'll join you later.'

Alicia and Jenny moved off along the scarred boards of the walk, heading for Mannix's store. Riddle glowered at Barradell and Merriam in seething silence until the sisters were out of earshot.

'Listen,' he grated at length, 'the Law and Order Committee elects peace officers here—'

'It doesn't,' interrupted Jeff Barradell. 'The marshal elects whom he pleases when it comes to picking deputies, the same as any marshal in any town. I'm marshal an' I see fit to elect Doctor Merriam. He's a sworn-in deputy an' he stays one until he wishes to resign or I fire him.'

'I'm chairman of the Law and Order Committee—' began Riddle, blustering, 'I'm chairman and—'

'And that don't mean you run this town, Riddle,' Barradell cut in icily. 'Yore committee wanted to get itself a gun-marshal, it got one, so leave him to do his own worryin' about his job. Good-morning!' Barradell strode off along the walk with tinkling spurs. Merriam offered the owner of the Rafter R a stiff little bow and walked after the marshal.

'Why, you—' snorted Riddle.

Barradell turned his head after walking some ten yards. The rancher was still standing by his buckboard, spluttering.

'I guess that told him,' murmured Merriam as they headed around the back of the big wooden bulk of the Southwest House to collect the doctor's horse.

'Guess it did,' granted Barradell. 'Seems Riddle wants

to have a big say in what goes on around this town, all right, but is he the big boss of the Border Bunch?'

'Not for my money,' Merriam commented. 'He hasn't the guts. If Riddle's in with them, he's being used by them.'

Ten minutes later, the two rode south out of town and were traversing the wide flats at a steady walk when they caught sight of an upward-swirling ribbon of distant dust.

'Riders – somewhere off over the rims!' Jeff Barradell said. They spurred up their animals and crested the rocky desert rims, keeping cautiously low in their saddles to prevent their being outlined against the azure sky.

Far below the rims, on a sand-carpeted flat which levelled away to the flat-summited mesas of the north, they saw perhaps two dozen riders. Distance-dwindled, they rode hastily northward, bundled close together, streamers of hoof-raised dust swirling high in their wake. And they were riding northward from the very direction in which lay that red sandstone wall and the tract of red sand which seemed ever-recurring in the trail of the Border Bunch.

'The Border Bunch!' exclaimed Merriam. 'It can't be anyone else! They're white men, not Indians, and only the Border Bunch would ride around here in force, but where are they headed?'

Barradell watched the clouds of dust raised by the distant riders float high on the crystal morning air, with his eyes narrowed against the brilliance of a sun only slightly dimmed by the approach of winter.

'No tellin',' he answered, 'unless our friend Albertson, over on Conquistadore Rim, knows the answer – if he isn't riding with them, that is!'

Silently, the pair watched the cluster of riders disappear around the face of a rearing butte away to the north. The floating haze of dust lingered long after their disappearance.

Barradell and Merriam spurred their mounts, came down the dusty rise of the rim, and lengthened the animals' stride off across the flat in the direction of the purple-misted bulk, high against the sky, which the medico pointed out as Conquistadore Rim.

Thirty minutes of steady hoofing brought them to the first upsweep of the high rim and they paced their mounts up it easily. Presently, they caught sight of the glittering water-hole and the weatherbeaten cabin standing beside it. The sun touched scatterings of trash around the door with stark light, underlining the squalor that the hand of man had brought to an otherwise pleasant location.

There was no sign of life from the cabin.

Barradell's sharp eyes caught sight of the unmistakable tracks and droppings of cattle angling up one side of the rim and off alongside the waterhole whose hoof-pocked edges betrayed the fact that many beeves on the hoof had watered here.

'Just as I thought. This place is used as a stop-over for stolen cattle, likely being driven to markets in New Mexico or Colorado. That's why they keep Albertson on this waterhole, I guess, to guard it an' keep it for Border Bunch use.'

Merriam indicated some dark scars on the ground close to a grove of live-oaks off to one side of the small *tinaja*.

'They've had fires there – branding fires, so they could change the irons on the cattle before they moved to more thickly populated regions.'

'Yeah. Seems to be a regular Border Bunch camp, this—' the marshal of Santa Rita began. He was cut off in mid-sentence as Merriam ducked low in his saddle and hissed a warning:

'Look out! A shot-gun!'

Barradell flattened himself against his gelding's neck in a quick reflex action. The instant he did so the bellowing blast of a shot-gun sounded from the cabin window and the slug went screeching over the head of the marshal.

Barradell's gun came out of its leather with a swift grab and the fractious gelding, scared by the sudden slam of the shot-gun, responded nervously as he yanked the rein with his free hand, pulling the animal off for the live-oak grove.

'Make for the oaks!' hissed Barradell.

Merriam was already acting, yanking his horse about and setting its nose for the oaks. Just as they pounded into the trees, another blast came from the cabin and a shell slashed through the winter-bare branches.

'He's a blamed lousy shot!' commented Barradell through clenched teeth.

'But that first one was near,' conceded Merriam. 'I saw the sun glitter on the barrel of his gun just before he fired.'

In the stand of live-oaks they tethered their horses and crouched low with ready guns. Though the spindly trees were winter-stark, they offered some cover, implemented by a slight knoll between the grove and the cabin. Crouching low in the coarse grass which grew between the trees, Barradell and Merriam could see the window of the cabin facing them and the big bulk of Albertson behind it holding a shot-gun prodded through a ragged break in the glass of the single, dirty pane. They saw the big Texan sway slightly and he appeared to be regarding the grove immediately opposite the cabin with an unsteady gaze.

Up against the azure sweep of the sky, the rusted stovepipe was slanted, a pungent smoke issuing from it. Barradell had noted the peculiar greyness of that thin ribbon of smoke when he first arrived on Conquistadore Rim and the sharp and acrid scent of it stung his nostrils bringing realization of what caused the smoke.

'Moonshine!' he sniffed. 'That galoot's operatin' a rotgut whiskey still in there!'

'So that's what he does to pass away his time,' remarked the gun-slinging medico. 'By the way the big oaf is acting, I'd say he was as drunk as a coot.'

'Good thing he is, otherwise he might not have missed us with that shot-gun at such close range,' Barradell murmured.

'How do we get him out of there?' Merriam grunted. 'He can pick us off the moment we stick our noses out of this grove, even if he is drunk!'

Jeff Barradell considered the thin plume of smoke

rising from the stove-pipe atop the cabin.

'I have a notion that might work if I can make a run from here to the cabin without that big ape plugging me. Keep me covered, Merriam, I'll try and make it.'

'What kind of crazy idea have you got in your head?' Merriam wanted to know.

'Just a hunch that I can get Albertson out of there alive an' able to tell us what we want to know.'

Before the doctor received an answer from Barradell's lips, the marshal of Santa Rita sprang into action. With his cocked six-gun in hand, hurtling forward in a half-crouch, he crashed through the live-oaks and the scrub which grew around their boles, heading directly for the open space between the grove and the rustler's cabin.

'The crazy coot!' snorted Merriam to himself as he watched the lean, range-clad figure go pounding up the slope of the little knoll.

Butch Albertson appeared at the small window, the sunshine putting a glitter on the barrel of his shot-gun. Barradell was clear of the grove of oaks now, his legs working like pistons, carrying him towards the shack at his lunging half-crouch, Albertson levelled the shot-gun. Barradell swerved off to one side.

Crouching in the grove, Merriam pegged a slug from his Smith & Wesson at the window, shattering the wood of the frame into flying shards and causing Albertson to jump back in alarm before triggering his weapon.

Barradell was still streaking for the small wooden building, his pounding boots scuffing up feathers of dust as he ran. He was close now, angling across towards the blind end of the cabin, away from the single window.

The unsteady form of the man in the cabin appeared once more at the window, glowering out towards the grove and flourishing the shot-gun. He snorted stupidly, unable to see the figure of the running man or the one in the grove of oaks.

Barradell was out of the window's view now, at the far gable end of the cabin where the rusted chimney spouted its ribbon of acrid smoke.

In the grove, Merriam was watching the marshal closely and in bewilderment.

'What in blazes is that fellow doing?' he asked himself. 'He's starting to climb the side of the cabin!'

TEN

Barradell was indeed climbing the side of the cabin, hauling himself up to the roof, finding purchase for his fingers and toes in the crevices between the logs.

Albertson was still staring wonderingly out of the window and the gunfighting doctor contemplated Barradell's climb to the cabin roof with equal wonderment. Moving swiftly, the marshal of Santa Rita reached the edge of the roof and slithered on to the heat-warped boards on his stomach. He eased himself into a sitting position and, with a certain waggish air, removed his sombrero and calmly placed it over the mouth of the stove-pipe out of which issued the pungent smoke of the rye-mash from which Butch Albertson was coaxing rotgut whiskey.

Hidden in the grove, George Merriam smiled.

'Well, the cunning *hombre* isn't crazy after all!' he told himself. 'He's smoking Albertson out! Once that smoke from the still starts to fill the cabin, even a Texas constitution won't stand up to it!'

Jeff Barradell, sitting on the cabin roof, waved his

hand with that waggishness which Merriam had never suspected was a part of the make-up of the lean, grim-featured reputation-pushing gunhand.

Several minutes passed in silence during which the features of the befuddled Albertson glowered from the cabin window two or three times. Then, a dribble of slate-grey thin smoke floated from the jagged hole in the window pane and a harsh cough spluttered inside the cabin. More smoke puffed from the window and the coughing came again, louder and of longer duration. Barradell's hat, firmly planted over the mouth of the tin chimney, was causing the pungent smoke to fill the cabin and the burly Texan therein was finding it discomforting.

Thicker volumes of smoke began to pour from the hole in the window and Butch Albertson was hacking and spluttering in extreme discomfort. Barradell edged along the roof until he was positioned directly over the door.

Suddenly, the sun-split door burst open and Albertson lurched out, spluttering, trailing his shot-gun and with billows of acrid smoke swirling about him.

The instant he appeared in the open, gasping for breath, the man on the roof launched himself forward, landing square on his shoulders, sending the rustler to the ground and his weapon skittering across the dust. Merriam came out of the oak-grove as Barradell was helping the spluttering, dust-spitting Texan to his feet, prodding his Colt into Albertson's ample stomach.

'That was a smart move.' praised Merriam. 'I guess you smoked this jack-rabbit out of his hole for sure.'

Butch Albertson was as much under the influence of his own brand of rotgut as he was under the influence of the pungent smoke. He swayed, coughing and gurgling colourful observations concerning the pair who covered him with their pistols.

'Now, Albertson, let's hear you talk,' said Barradell, jabbing the cow-thief in the region of his belt-buckle with his Colt.

Albertson spluttered a curse.

'First thing we want to know is why Claffin an' that cowhand were shot at the Rafter R,' the marshal told the big Texan. 'Then we want to know who shot them and who the big boss of the Border Bunch is and where they hole up.'

Albertson spat into the dust.

'The hell you do,' he mouthed drunkenly. 'You won't find out from me!'

Albertson was far gone in his cups and water streamed from his smoke-tortured eyes; nevertheless, he put up a show of bold bluster.

'Better talk, Butch,' Merriam advised quietly. 'We're in no mood for fooling. We want to know one or two things – like where those Border Bunch riders were headed for when they rode north in a bundle.'

'Border Bunch riders goin' north?' echoed Albertson dully. 'What're you talkin' about?'

An expression of enlightenment settled on his face all at once and he gave a hooting chuckle. 'So they was headed north was they?' he grinned foolishly, lurching in a tangle-footed fashion. 'Too late for you to do anythin' about them, Mister Smart-Alecky Marshal,' he snorted, addressing Barradell. 'It's the Tucson trail for them an' they'll grab that bullion consignment out of Bisbee long before it gets within miles of Tucson!' He clapped a broad hand over his mouth as if realizing that he had said too much.

'Bisbee? Bullion?' repeated Barradell, jabbing the mouth of his Colt deeper into Butch Albertson's paunch. 'Talk, Albertson! Talk, *muy pronto*! What mine is this load comin' from – talk quick!'

'I don't know,' quavered Albertson. 'Honest, I don't know anythin' more'n that – Claffin told me when he stopped by here.'

'Stopped by on his way over from Tombstone, I suppose,' reasoned Jeff Barradell. 'That's why he was loafin' around the Tombstone region – takin' a look-see at what loot was in the offin' for the Border Bunch to grab. What else do you know, Albertson? Speak up, or I'll ventilate you!'

The big Texan was shivering visibly.

'I don't know nothin' else, honest – don't ask me! The boss'll kill me!'

'The boss – who's the boss?' persisted Barradell, making a threatening move with his six-gun.

'Don't ask me,' quavered the jittery Albertson. 'I can't tell you!'

Merriam intervened.

'We won't get anything out of this guy, he's too drunk and scared to talk straight but, if it's true that the Border Bunch is headed for the Tucson trail to lay up for the bullion load from Bisbee, we might have time to get over there and intervene.'

'The boss'll kill me,' mouthed the big Texan stupidly. 'He'll kill me for sure.'

'You're right, Merriam,' Barradell conceded grimly. 'We might make it if we ride like blazes. There's no time to gather a posse, so we'll have to go alone.'

'A posse!' repeated the medico with obvious disgust. 'Only people we can raise around here to form a posse are those in that milk-and-water law and order outfit back at Santa Rita – there's no time to head back there, anyway.'

Barradell turned to Albertson.

'The best thing for you is to pack yore warsack and ride plumb out of this country,' he advised. 'Hit the trail for Mexico or California, get out of Arizona and consider yoreself a lucky man. Don't let me see you anywhere around these parts while I'm totin' a law-star! '

The Texan was deathly white and teetering unsteadily on his high-heeled cow-wrangler's boots.

'I'm goin',' he husked. 'I'm goin', all right. The boss'll gun me down for spillin' the beans if I don't haze out of here pronto!'

He started an erratic progression in the direction of the cabin. Barradell watched him go, keeping an eye peeled for any attempt on the Texas rustler's part to make a grab for the shot-gun lying in the dust and scatterings of litter by the door of the building. Albertson, in a stupefied daze, walked right past it and entered the still smoke-filled cabin.

Barradell climbed to the roof once more and retrieved his hat from the smoke-stack. Jamming it on his head, he joined Merriam.

'I'd like to push that question as to who's bossin' the

Border Bunch down his ear three or four times more,' the marshal commented as the pair walked towards the grove where their horses were tethered.

Swiftly, they mounted and took their animals down the sweep of Conquistadore Rim. They rode steadily at a lope for an hour, traversing the desert flats where gigantic sandstone monuments raised their wind-eroded bulks against the sun-washed sky and long-armed saguaro cactus stood on parade with yucca, Spanish dagger and a hundred and one varieties of thorny scrub cluttering about them.

They came to a water-hole, watered and rested their animals, then pressed silently onward, two madly-travelling mounted figures against the barren vastness of the desert.

Their horses flagged, but the riders spurred them mercilessly. They rode over rims, across flats and alkali-sinks. Away on the horizon, blued by distance, stood the mountain fastnesses of the Huachucas and Dragoons. The winter-edged wind came keening down across the desert floor, whipping flurries of stinging sand against men and horses.

'Blamed wind,' grunted Barradell, as the pair hoofed over a wide flat. 'It's blowin' sand about so any tracks the Border Bunch left have been covered.'

'Tucson trail's over towards the east,' Merriam stated, 'we'll hit it in an hour or so.'

They took their wearied horses over the tumbled land, urging every ounce of energy out of them. The barren miles flew into their back-trail as they pounded onwards.

Presently, they rimmed a high upsweep of scrub-topped sand and saw the garish ribbon of the Tucson trail snaking over the flat far below. For an instant they yanked rein to give the horses a blow, but the far clatter of a gun, followed rapidly by a second shot galvanized them into action.

Barradell kicked spurs into his gelding, prodding the animal into headlong speed.

'C'mon,' he roared to his partner. 'They're down there in the sage by the twist in the trail!'

Merriam put his mount into neck-stretching speed, thundering down the side of the rise in a cloud of dust and clawing for his Smith & Wesson as he went. He saw the trail below and tiny puffs of blue smoke rising from a green and brown clutter of sagebrush into which the trail to Tucson twisted. Indistinct, horse-back-high figures were moving in the sage and the distance-thinned bark of guns sounded continuously.

Barradell and Merriam reached the flat and set their animals to hurtling across the alkali-dusted sand. Drawing closer to the fight on the trail, they saw a bobbing cluster of riders, all with their faces masked with squares of black cloth, slamming lead at the defenders of two sack-loaded wagons. A third wagon had been pulled clear of the others and was in the possession of a trio of masked desperados who were urging its team off the trail and on to the desert flat.

Through the swirls of gunsmoke they saw three bullion-haulers to each wagon, lying among the sacks, trying to repel the robbers, while four more of their kind lay dead in the dust.

'Those wagon fellows are outnumbered,' yelled Barradell against the rush of the wind. 'Let's go in there smokin'!'

They reached the ribbon of the trail and came upon the robbers with pistols spitting lead and fire and making their shots tell. With their furious arrival on the scene, the black-masked Border Bunch marauders stiffened in their saddles and pitched down to the dust.

In the choking, hoof-pounded dust and the wreaths of cordite smoke, the saddle-bandits circling the bullion wagons turned about to meet the threat of the newly-arrived pair. In bellowing, dust- and smoke-hazed fury, a tall, black-clad and double-gunned masked rider was barking orders in a harsh voice, urging his men to pack themselves in around the wagons to meet the gun-spitting pair who came trigger-tripping on pounding hooves from the desert flats.

The big boss! thought Barradell as he split the breeze with his head ducked low and his six-gun bucking. *That's the big boss of the bunch! He ain't Riddle, whoever he is!*

A thundering hell of action boiled around the bullion wagons on the trail; horses snorted and pranced high to the blast of gunfire. The marshal of Santa Rita and his partner were suddenly in the thick of it, tossing in their saddles in the upward-fanning puffs of dust, their pistols spitting out flames of death.

The arrival of the lead-throwing pair injected a new vigour into the defenders of the wagons. Their Winchesters lanced out white flames of muzzle-fire as they pumped shells into the breeches and fired continuously.

Barradell became separated from Merriam. His horse lurched under him in the bellowing and oddly timeless turmoil raging around the wagons. Black-masked figures were dropping from their saddles, bullets zipped around his head like angry leaden hornets. He caught sight of Merriam, his mount yanked in close to the wagons. A wide, devil-may-care grin was on the neatly bearded face of the gunslinging medico and his Winchester had replaced his Smith & Wesson in his hands.

Jeff Barradell's hat was carried away by a whanging slug as he was in the act of triggering the last round from the chamber of his six-gun. He shoved the Colt into its holster and clawed his repeater from the saddle-scabbard under his knee. Crouching low over his gelding's neck, he fired, pumped, and fired again into the dust and smoke-hazed mêlée of vague, dark-masked phantom shapes.

The vicious snarl of a bullet sounded an inch from his ear and he felt its hot scorch fan past his face. The gelding kicked its forelegs high, then suddenly dropped limply under the saddle as a bullet took it square in the head. Barradell saw the chaotic panorama of the gun-fight fly upward past his eyes as he went sprawling from the saddle. A sixth sense spurred him as he hurtled downwards and he launched his body off to one side, clutching his rifle close to him and curling his knees up to his chest so that he would not be trapped under the weight of the dead animal.

He smote the dust shoulder-on and sprawled there panting for breath. Smoking, blasting action rolled around him, hooves tramped and showered hot grit across his face. He came up to his knees and blasted the Winchester time and again into the thick of the Border Bunch desperados.

Somewhere, it seemed another world away, a voice yipped:

'They're pullin' off, by grab! They're runnin' for it!'

Down in the dust, Barradell. was aware that the hooves of the Border Bunch horses were drawing back from the wagons. He heard the harsh voice of the double-gunned leader, the mysterious big boss, roaring for his men to pull back.

'Licked, by the great horned toad,' enthused the voice from the wagons. 'They're pullin' back! We gave 'em enough fight!'

Down in the swirling dust, the marshal of Santa Rita was aware of ghostly, haze-curtained riders yanking their animals about and setting their noses for the wilderness.

Dust clogged his eyes and sweat streaked down from his brow in rivulets. He settled back on his heels, the Winchester clamped to his shoulder, and emptied the magazine at the retreating robbers who were turned about in their leather, slamming parting shots at the defenders of the wagons.

'Just a few,' he gritted, 'on behalf of Al Poindexter!'

ELEVEN

The battle subsided with the Border Bunch marauders hazing off into the desert with plumes of dust fanning wide in their back-trail.

Barradell picked himself up wearily and made his way to the clutter of bullion wagons. Merriam was there, sitting his saddle impatiently, his Winchester smoking across his knees. The doctor was watching the dwindling saddle-bandits pounding off over the flat to join the stolen bullion wagon which their partners in crime were taking southward, whipping up the team to neck-stretching speed.

'I've half a mind to go after them,' Merriam growled.

'Take it easy,' counselled the marshal, dashing perspiration from his brow. 'You've got the only saddle-horse among us an' you couldn't do anythin' against that crew on yore own!'

'It riles me to see them get away with that wagon,' Merriam admitted.

'Sure, but one wagon is all they got, we kept off the others.'

The leader of the bullion-haulers, a stocky man with a scrubby beard, came down from the top of one of the vehicles.

'Sure was mighty handy you comin' along when you did,' he said gratefully. 'That crowd of hellions jumped us before we knew where we was. Just seemed to come up out of the desert like gophers comin' outa their holes.'

'Yeah;' Barradell grunted. 'The Border Bunch is some tough outfit all right.' He surveyed the black-masked bodies scattered about the wagons. 'I guess we gave them a tolerable fight, though. That wagonload of bullion was bought at a high cost – pity we didn't get the big boss, whoever he is.'

'He got clear away;' replied one of the waggoners who was dabbing at a bullet-nicked ear with his bandanna. 'I saw him whoopin' an' hollerin' for the rest of the bunch to hightail for the desert.'

'I'd give a mighty lot,' murmured the marshal, watching the distance-lessened forms of the Border Bunch riders moving up a rim, 'to know just who that *hombre* is.'

'I guess we'll find out one day – or the Border Bunch'll put us where we won't feel inquisitive.' Merriam answered. 'Pass me the canteen from your horse, some of these men have wounds that need cleaning out.'

'How many men have you lost?' Barradell asked the team captain.

'Five. Four of us are shot up, but not badly.'

'Why didn't yore company send out a bigger number of men? You need a powerful strong shot-gun guard on bullion trains with this Border Bunch runnin' around.'

'We figured we was strong enough – but we would have been swamped only for you two comin' along.'

'It was our duty to come along, we're peace officers. I'm marshal of Santa Rita.'

Jeff Barradell saw the team leader's eyes widen.

'Oh, yeah.' he said, 'we've heard of you.'

Barradell knew what they'd heard. That Jeff Barradell, the gunman who turned in his partner, had come to take the place of Al Poindexter, that other gunhawk tarred with exactly the same brush.

'The name,' he said slowly, contemplating the wagon-team captain with bleak eyes, 'is Smith!' He felt the futility of it all as he spoke. They knew who he was, the whole country around here knew who he was. Hadn't Jenny, Riddle's younger daughter, told him so when she dressed the bullet-nick in his arm?

'Oh,' said the wagon-hauler. 'Marshal Smith.'

Barradell paid no attention. He was thinking of Jenny and the way the scornful words fell from her delicate lips, bringing such strange pain to a nature which he long thought hardened against the sting of hard words. She had courage to talk that way to his kind, though, for she had no way of knowing how he'd react to her derision. Many another of his kind would have shown their resentment more forcibly than by the sarcastic words he'd loosed on her. 'Billy the Kid' Bonney, who was usually courteous towards women, would have slapped her across the mouth for that kind of talk, so would Wes Hardin.

She was a plucky kid, all right; pretty and plucky with a spirit he admired.

Barradell tore himself away from thoughts of the girl, inwardly berating himself.

'We better bury the dead Border Bunch gunnies here on the desert,' he advised. 'Then you'd best take yore wagons an' yore own dead into Tombstone, that's nearer than turnin' back to Bisbee. Your men will be decently buried in Boot Hill.'

'Maybe we could get a posse raised in Tombstone an' go out after those hellions,' suggested the wagon-captain.

Barradell shook his head. 'They have too good a start. Merriam an' I will have to track 'em alone, but you'll have to give me one of yore team-horses to ride. Report what happened here to the sheriff of Cochise County when you reach Tombstone. This is rightly his jurisdiction.'

Merriam concluded dressing the wounds of the teamsters in the rough and ready way which was the only one possible and the lawmen and wagon-haulers set about burying the Border Bunch gunmen who had died following their desperate mode of life. They whipped the black silk squares from the faces of the corpses and Barradell gasped at the sight of two of them.

'Gent Grex and Lafe Channing!' he whistled. 'So that's what happened to that pair; they threw their guns in with the Border Bunch!'

'And this,' commented George Merriam, studying another unmasked corpse, 'is Rudd Walsh, who built himself a gun-reputation in Colorado. I remember seeing him in Denver once.'

Barradell considered the dead men. Three of them were men with quick trigger reputations and a fourth with an equally big score of notches on the barrel of his six-gun came to tell him that the mysterious big boss would welcome his trigger skill in the Border Bunch ranks only the day before. So the boss of the saddle-bandits had made up his crew of big-name gunfighters – and he doubtless approached Al Poindexter with the same proposition, then bush-whacked him because he really had changed his spots.

So, this was what he was up against and this was what Poindexter had been up against: a renegade outfit made up of gunnies who had lone-hawked it along the dim-trails for year after bullet-torn year and had now banded themselves together in a death-deal-ing, plundering company of raiders led by an unknown, black-clad man who brandished two guns.

Barradell thought constantly of that man as he helped with laying the Border Bunch gunmen into the ignominious, unmarked desert graves they had earned. He saw him again in his mind's eye, that lean, gun-blasting figure, bucking in his saddle against the chaotic backcloth of battle, anonymous behind the black cloth under the black sombrero.

Someday, he'd know who he was.

The early afternoon found Barradell and his part-ner striking off to the south in the wake of the Border

Bunch, having left the wagon teams to make their way to Tombstone.

Barradell was mounted on one of the tough team animals, not built for speed, but possessing considerable strength.

On the barren rims, they picked up the trail of the Border Bunch – hoof-pocks in a trampled ribbon and the wheel-scores of the stolen bullion-wagon visible in a hollow on the far side of the rims where the winter-edged wind had not disturbed the sand.

'Heading directly south,' Barradell commented. 'Hightailin' for their hidey-hole, I guess.'

'Or Mexico,' the medico answered. 'That's where they'd dispose of the loot without a lot of trouble.'

Slapping their knees against the ribs of their mounts, they urged the animals onward across the windswept flats. The going was hard. The animal between Barradell's legs was no saddle-horse and Merriam's mount was weary. Mile after wilderness mile passed under the southward plodding hooves. The westering sun touched a ruddy glow to the sky, there was no sign to follow after the sheltered lee of the rim, but the pair kept riding doggedly onward over scrub-dotted, cactus-guarded miles.

Suddenly, a plume of drifting smoke took the attention of George Merriam. He pointed to it excitedly.

'See that? Off to the south-west – smoke!'

Barradell followed the direction of his companion's pointing arm and saw the blue feather of the smoke drifting up against the blood-tinged purple of the high sky.

'Maybe they're makin' camp at a water-hole,' he suggested. 'Let's get over there, fast, but cautious!'

Their progression was as fast as they could make it on jaded animals and, when they topped a rise, they saw it was no camp-fire that caused the ribbon of smoke. Down on the desert floor, the remains of the bullion-wagon were blazing; the wheel-rims and the broad metal axle-shafts were clearly visible in the midst of the still blazing heap of rubble. Barradell and Merriam rode down the rise and considered the burning vehicle. Most of it was rendered to blackened laths and planks but the fire was still ablaze, proving it was started but a short time before.

'Burned the wagon and took the bullion on without it, eh?' Barradell said, half to himself. 'Probably usin' the team-horses as pack-animals.'

'Funny thing to do, burn a wagon,' Merriam observed. 'It left a mighty plain pointer as to their direction.'

Barradell contemplated the ground around the burning wagon. The wind which had fanned the flames into a quickly-spreading and hungry fire had scoured the desert floor clean of any hoofprints to point to the direction taken by the desperados.

'Maybe it's too plain a pointer,' he growled. 'They could have dumped the wagon without burnin' it if it was cumbersome. Settin' it alight that way could have been a deliberate way of bringin' us off the trail.'

'You mean some of them brought the wagon over here and burned it, knowing its smoke would bring us in this direction, while the rest of the bunch hightailed off in another direction?' Merriam asked.

'Sure, just that,' the marshal agreed.

Merriam narrowed his eyes and studied the far-stretching wilderness.

'Come to think of it, this is a long way off the direction to either Santa Rita or the place where you think the Border Bunch might have its hiding-hole, though it would lead to the Mexico line if you kept on moving south,' mused the medico. 'Only point a group of travellers might make for from here would be the Silla Blanco water-hole over to the south-east.'

'Let's head for it,' Barradell suggested. 'They likely put this burnin' wagon here as a fooler, so we'd follow its smoke an' lose their trail somewhere around nightfall. They timed it pretty well, too, it ain't far from dusk now.'

Already, the purple shadows of the fast-falling wilderness night were sifting over the far rises of the high buttes and the ragged lines of the Huachucas at their back.

'Our horses need water, anyway,' Merriam said. 'Silla Blanco is the place to head for.'

They angled off across the flat, traversing streaks of alkali dust and silica deposits. The night wind swept the desert with a breath touched with the chill of approaching winter; high in the dark-purple vault of the night, speckled with the bright dots of the stars, a white moon rode, silvering the stark land. Riding their wearied horses easily over the moonlight-sharpened barrens for almost an hour from the point where they found the burning wagon, the pair reached the Silla

Blanco water-hole. The oasis was deserted, a moon-glit-tered sheet of water in a setting of sun-blasted rocks, one of them wind-eroded to the semblance of a saddle – the white saddle which gave the *tinaja* its name.

Gratefully, Barradell and Merriam watered their horses, drank their own fill and replenished their big desert canteens. Close to the water's edge, they found boot- and hoof-prints as well as the butts of recently smoked ricepaper cigarettes.

'They stopped here,' the marshal mused. 'So burn-ing that wagon was just a fooler to take us off their track. They're takin' the bullion south without the wagon, which means they can't be movin' fast with that weight on their cayuses, but they can still go faster than us because our horses are tired by that needless detour.'

'We'll have to rest them, Barradell, any more push-ing on and mine'll drop dead under me.'

They rested at the water-hole, leaning back against the rocks, smoking and thinking of the saddle-bandits already on their way south with the stolen bullion.

Merriam considered the trail-wearied features of his partner, lean and hollowed in the white rays of the moon.

'You're a strange man to understand, Barradell,' he observed.

Barradell started, his thoughts torn away from the Border Bunch.

'No less strange than your own self,' he answered. 'What brought this on?'

'I was considering your doggedness in going after

those renegades,' the bearded medico said. 'You really
hate lawbreakers, don't you – in spite of what they say
about you?'

'You mean in spite of havin' been one myself an'
turnin' in a partner so I would be given a free pardon?'
the marshal replied. 'All right, Merriam – your story
for mine.'

Merriam pulled back his lips into a hard smile. He
gazed at the moon-sheened water of the oasis with
bitter eyes, remembering something.

'How I got this way? It's a short story, Barradell,
something that happened in the east not many years
ago when I was newly qualified. I operated on a man
and he died – because I was falling down drunk when
I performed the operation.' He picked up a small
pebble and hurled it into the water-hole. Its *plop* was
a note of finality and moon-touched circles raced
across the surface of the water.

'The man was my brother,' Merriam said bitterly.

Barradell nodded. He saw now why this man was
running to seed in a fly-eaten border-town. There were
many such on the frontier – men who were escaping
from something, men who rode west with bitter memories and who rarely found the peace they sought.

'So you came west,' Barradel murmured.

'Yes – west to the whiskey bottle, the playing-cards
and the six-gun, watching myself run to seed, knowing
I'm too good a man to go to seed and knowing that only
a firm hand can stop me. I mean a woman's firm hand,
Barradell, and there's only one woman in the world
who could tame me down.'

Jeff Barradell grunted, thinking of Charlie Riddle's daughter, Alicia. She wasn't his kind, cold and haughty as she appeared to be, but maybe she was exactly the kind of woman who might tone this wild medico down to the level of respectability on which he belonged. Her sister, now, Jenny, maybe she was nearer his own kind – a spirited little firebrand who wasn't afraid to say her say.

Merriam watched the marshal of Santa Rita with inquiring eyes, waiting for him to come through with his side of the bargain.

'That story about my selling out a partner,' Barradell told him, 'it just isn't true. I know a lot of gunslingers have pulled rewards off their heads by turning over their partners and then put a tin-star on their vests, but in my case it wasn't like that.

'It happened in Nebraska four or five years back, after the US marshals shot up the Split Boulder rustler outfit. I was runnin' with the Split Boulder crowd because a big rancher back home in Nevada – one of Riddle's kind an' the man whose outfit ruined my father's horse-ranch – put the outlaw brand on me so good that I couldn't get an honest job no-how. The Split Boulder bunch broke up – at least, what was left of the outfit after the law shot up its hide-out, broke up – we had to run for all points of the compass at once. One of them was mighty badly shot up in the leg, so bad that none of the others would have him along with them 'cause he'd hinder them in hightailin' for the tall timber. He was no friend of mine, but I couldn't leave an injured man for the hang-rope, so I let him tag on to me. We started sloggin' south, the two of us on dead beat horses an' the whole country was alive with marshals an' vigilantes. We had to travel at night, holin' up in the daytime, findin' water when we were lucky an' doin' without food.

'My partner's leg was givin' him hell an' I decided we'd head for a small town where we might find a doctor to patch it up at gun-point. We got close to the town at dawn. Just as we approached the main trail into the place, we saw dozens of vigilantes an' marshals ridin' in. They somehow got on to our trail an' figured we might ride for that town. My partner an' I bedded down in some timber off the trail to wait the day out an' hope the law would move off elsewhere. I was just about all in for want of food an' rest an' I guess I fell asleep from sheer exhaustion. When I woke, the sun was pretty high an' my partner an' both horses were missin'. Then I saw a heap of mounted men comin' up the slopes to the timber where I was holed-up – with the guy I'd helped leadin' them. He'd sneaked away to the town, takin' both horses, while I was asleep, to turn me into the law so he'd get himself a pardon.

'They got me cornered an' I gunned it out as far as I could, keepin' on the run through the timber. That wood was alive with marshals an' vigilantes an' I kept dodgin' through the scrub an' the brush. I gave 'em the slip for a while but then I heard someone hollerin' for help an' found my Split Boulder partner thrown from the fresh horse the law gave him an' bawling for help. His fine friends of the law were so busy lookin' for me they left him on the ground whoopin' – after all, he'd served his purpose in leadin' them to my hidin' hole.

'He begged me to help him. I didn't. I left him there for the attentions of his law an' order friends an' took his horse. After a while, I got clear away an' plumb out of Nebraska. I guess the story that I turned my partner in for a pardon just naturally got around, but I didn't. The fact is there's still a Nebraska warrant hangin' over me. I made it to Texas an' took to law an' order – I was through with owl-hootin'.'

Barradell jerked the butt of his rice-paper smoke from his taut lips and crushed it into the sand with his thumb by way of putting a full stop to his story.

Merriam said:

'The horses are rested enough. Let's ride.'

TWELVE

The leader of the Border Bunch was in a distinctly ugly mood as he and his robber-outfit moved south over the barrens. The robbers had suffered much in the attack on the bullion consignment into which Barradell and Merriam had intervened with such deadly effect.

Several of the masked riders – the picked, reputation-pushing gunmen – were wounded. The going was slow, for the horses were weary and carrying the weight of the stolen bullion sacks in addition to their riders.

Riding sullenly at the head of his column of renegades, the masked, black-clad outlaw leader with his twin Colts glittering in the ornately tooled holsters thonged against his thighs, considered the gun-spitting fury of the two who came haring off the desert. In his mind, dark formulations began to take shape. The coming of Barradell – Barradell of the shady reputation who had obviously not changed his spots – to Santa Rita, was a disaster to the Border Bunch. The leader of the outlaw faction had tried to secure his gun-skill and failed – and his messenger had been planted in an unmarked grave on Santa Rita's cemetery hill. Barradell and Merriam had become symbols of ruin to the man who had built up the Border Bunch by the devilish cunning of well-laid plans. There would have to be a showdown and the pair would have to be killed.

The outlaws rode wearily over the moon-washed wilderness landscape, some of them nursing wounds, all muttering and grumbling.

Their leader was aware of the ugly humour in his men and the fact that they needed food and drink and their wounds attending to. As the string of masked riders rode under the lip of a high butte, the leader swung his mount over to the west.

'Hey! We should move east if we're headed back for the hole!' objected one of the riders at his back.

'We ain't headed for the hole,' the leader told him curtly.

'Oh, we're goin' right on over the border, so we can get rid of this loot, huh?' asked the outlaw.

'Not immediately,' the Border Bunch leader answered. 'You men need rest an' food an' those wounds cleanin' up. Ain't much in the way of good food an' medical supplies back at the hole, so we're headin' for the Rafter R – then the border!'

'The Rafter R!' exploded another of the bunch. 'But there's a bunch of cowhands on the place – Riddle might be runnin' with us, but his men ain't an' we ain't in good fightin' trim to invade the place.'

'Cowhands!' scorned the outlaw leader. 'A bunch of branders an' ropers is all Riddle has on his outfit – none of 'em are fightin' men. We can handle those *hombres* if anyone objects to us showin' up. We can rest there awhile, then push on to Mexico.'

The men at his back grunted their approval; they were weary and injured and this sounded a good proposition. Doggedly, bearing the looted sacks over their saddle-pommels, they wound over the wilderness miles.

'Won't be any danger from Barradell an' his sawbones friend,' observed the boss of the Border Bunch with satisfaction. 'That notion of takin' the wagon a few miles off the trail an' burnin' it has likely confused 'em as to our direction. When we meet up with that pair again, there'll be hell to pay for sure. Meantime, it's the Rafter R for us, then the border.'

Their progress was slow and the outlaw chief rode with his dark plans forming. Maybe, he thought, the only sure way to rid this country of Jeff Barradell and his gunslinging medico friend would be to go after them himself and smoke it out, gun to gun. Well, if it came to that, he'd do it. The Border Bunch was the solidification of a dream he'd nurtured for a long time – a big-time lawless outfit with himself as its brain. He'd brought it into being in this wild land and there was not room here for both his outlaw bunch and the marshal of Santa Rita or his upstart medico friend.

Under the opening gates of the new dawn, the Border Bunch came to Rafter R land and they reached the ranch headquarters while the tranquillity of sleep still held the place.

The ranch-house and the bunk-house were quiet and in darkness. The red shafts of dawn-light speared across the rutted yard and the chillness of winter was in the wind.

The outlaw leader pulled rein some distance from the ranch buildings.

'Picket yore horses here,' he told his men. 'Walk into the place with yore spurs off, we don't want to waken any of Riddle's ropers an' branders. If we can get into the ranch-house without raisin' any racket it'll be all the better. There'll only be Riddle and his daughters in there.'

The renegades draped their reins over the necks of their animals so they hung against their knees to prevent them from straying. They left the horses on the grassland and walked cautiously, minus ringing spurs, into the yard of the Rafter R.

'Three or four of you come with me,' the Border Bunch leader told his men, 'the rest of you keep yore eyes on the bunkhouse.'

He mounted the shadowy gallery with a handful of his men following. Cautiously, he tried the ranch-house door and it yielded under his touch.

'Riddle don't think there's any need to lock up his place at night,' he.murmured, 'that's lucky for us.'

His men followed him into the spacious living-room of the building, now lit only by the shafts of dawn-light which filtered through the windows, and the outlaw chief considered one of the doors leading off the room.

'That's Riddle's bedroom, if I remember the lay-out of this house properly,' observed the Border Bunch leader. 'Looks like Mr Big Rancher Riddle is due for a rude awakening.'

Riddle was indeed given a rude awakening. He woke to a rough hand shaking him forcefully and found a knot of black-clad, masked ghosts standing about his bed. He stared at the macabre figures in the dawn-lit room and his mouth began to form words:

'What're you doing here?' he squawked from the midst of his bedclothes. 'We agreed that you and your men should keep away from here!'

'Get up!' rasped the leader of the outlaw crew. 'This is one time we're payin' you a visit. My boys need wounds dressin' and food. Get yore daughters awake an' make 'em fix somethin'.'

Riddle began to protest, but the claw-like hand of the outlaw chief, moving for one of the glittering Colts at his thigh, caused his objections to die half-uttered.

'Move, *muy pronto*, Riddle;' grated the masked one. 'An' we don't want any interference from yore cow-chasers!

Meanwhile, off on the desert barrens, Jed Barradell and the wayward, gunslinging medical man came to the sheltered lee of the high, wind-torn butte. Here, the desert wind had not touched the shaly tract which spread under the butte and that tract of scrub-dotted desert floor was trampled by the unmistakable prints of heavily-laden horses – prints which turned off in a westward direction.

The mounted men sat their saddles in a long

minute of silence, their wilderness-trained eyes considering the tracks.

'Moving westward;' grunted Barradell, at length.

'Towards Riddle's ranch,' the doctor put in grimly. 'My guess is that's where we'll meet up with the Border Bunch and maybe we'll find out just what part Riddle plays in their set-up.'

They touched their spurs to the flanks of their animals and followed the westering trail.

Jed McAndrew, foreman of the Rafter R, issued his orders for the day's work right after breakfast when the golden disc of the sun was flooding the flawless sky with its glory. Having detailed the riders to the various jobs on the range, McAndrew held back four of them. There was a query as to whether the creek on the east pasture should be cleared of brushwood that had clogged it or whether a check should be made of the quicksand over on the south pasture. The wire fence around that sink hadn't looked any too safe last time he rode past and another fool cowcrittur might have barged through it and got herself swallowed up.

Jed McAndrew didn't know which was the most important chore. He'd ask the boss and detail these men to attend to whatever he thought needed priority attention.

Leaving the cowhands to blanket and saddle-up their range-ponies, he ambled off towards the ranch-house. An easy-going man was McAndrew, a capable cattleman, no fighting man but nobody's fool. As he approached the ranch-house, it came to him that he had seen nothing of Riddle or his two daughters that morning, but that was nothing unusual. Mounting the gallery steps, he thought he heard the harsh laugh of a man, a laugh he had never heard before, which ceased as soon as his boots tramped on the wood of the gallery with his spurs clicking.

Oddly, the door of the house swung open quickly and Charlie Riddle appeared, closing the door at his back and standing with his back pressed against it and holding the handle. His features were pale and his usual precise demeanour was replaced by an obvious jittery manner.

McAndrew was in the habit of walking into the house whenever he had business there, but it seemed as if Riddle had seen his approach from one of the windows and stepped out on to the gallery to prevent his entry.

Some mighty funny things were going on around this spread just lately, reflected Jed McAndrew. What with an unknown intruder shooting one of the cowboys and a prisoner the marshal was taking back to Santa Rita – in broad daylight when the marshal was on the ranch – and now the boss looking so obviously scared.

Riddle listened to his foreman's query with undisguised impatience, still standing with his back to the door, blocking McAndrew from any attempt to enter the house. His reply was hasty and the foreman's question seemed hardly considered:

'Er – attend to that quicksand fence, Jed. Make sure

it's strung with strong wire – can't risk losing any stock in that sink-hole.'

McAndrew nodded. Once again, he thought he heard the deep murmur of voices inside the ranch-house – men's voices – and it was evident from the rancher's behaviour that there was something, or someone, inside the house he did not want his foreman to know of.

It was darn funny, thought the foreman as he nodded assent to the orders of Charlie Riddle.

Jed McAndrew moved off, gathered his detachment of cowhands and they struck out for the south pasture. Clear of the ranch headquarters, they saw something that diverted their attention from the work in hand – a clutter of picketed horses and two unidentifiable riders sitting their saddles close to them.

The Rafter R wranglers turned their horses' noses for the far riders and the knot of grazing animals and found the riders to be the man who called himself Smith and who people said was really Jeff Barradell, the gunfighter, and the bearded, devil-be-damned doctor from Santa Rita.

It was the marshal of Santa Rita who spoke first.

'These Rafter R cayuses?' he hailed as the foreman and his party rode up.

'No, they ain't,' responded McAndrew, who knew every horse in the ranch's *remuda*. 'They're not our critters. Are they branded?'

'They ain't, but we don't need brands to tell who they belong to. They belong to the Border Bunch an' we believe some of those hellions are on yore outfit,' the marshal said bluntly. 'What do you know about the set-up?'

'The Border Bunch!' echoed the Rafter R punchers.

Jed McAndrew was silent, recalling the odd behaviour of Charlie Riddle and the half-heard voices of strange men issuing from the house.

'Yeah,' he said slowly. 'There is somethin' strange goin' on at the house – an' there's someone in there.'

'Then it's the Border Bunch gunnies an', whether you know it or not, yore boss is in with that outfit,' Barradell told the punchers. 'They have a load of bullion taken from a Bisbee consignment an' we aim to take 'em. Where do you fellows stand with the Border Bunch?'

Jed McAndrew made answer for the cowhands with him:

'We're against 'em!' he declared firmly. 'We ain't fightin' men, but we all have guns an' if we can help rid this territory of that blamed crew, we're with you, ain't we, boys?'

'Sure,' chorused the others.

'By grab!' rumbled one of the wranglers. 'The boss in with that outfit – I can't believe it!'

'All right,' urged Barradell, thumping the ribs of his horse with his knees. 'Let's go!'

In both Alicia and Jenny Riddle there was a horrified numbness.

Their home had been invaded by men with masked faces, men who now lay around on chairs, some even sprawled on the floor, sleeping heavily. Others sat by the curtained windows watching the outside world with wary eyes and ready guns.

On the floor lay the heavy sacks of loot they had brought with them. Their leader, now stretched wearily on a chair, seemed to have an evil hold over their father. Masked as he was, dressed in black, with two well-maintained six-guns holstered at his lean thighs, he seemed more phantom than mortal man and was, indeed, a phantom to the girls. The voice that spoke from behind the black square covering the face of the leader of the Border Bunch was a voice the girls knew from the past.

To bear it again was startling, numbing – horrifying.

On the orders of this voice they had been roused from their beds, forced to prepare a meal for the invaders of their home and dress their bullet-wounds.

Their father's protests were silenced by growls from the weary outlaws and their evil, phantom-like leader. The outlaws declared their intention of waiting until they were rested, then moving on. Alicia and Jenny hoped and prayed they would soon move on or that the Rafter R hands would return from the ranges unexpectedly to intervene. This last was a vain half-hope. The cow-wranglers were scarcely fighting men and would be a poor match for these gun-hung border renegades.

One of the masked outlaws squatting by a window suddenly started and growled an oath.

The tramp of hooves came from the ranch-yard. As if a sixth-sense, developed by years on the owl-hoot trails warned him, the black-garbed phantom who led the outlaws sprang up from his chair. He moved to the heavily curtained window with the speed of a pouncing mountain-lion.

'What is it?' he demanded.

'That Barradell an' Merriam an' a bundle of other galoots!' snorted the bandit, grabbing for his six-gun as he made answer. 'The whole bunch of them, ridin' into the yard!'

Charlie Riddle swept his daughters back to the far wall of the room, out of range of the window.

'Get back and stay back!' he told them, his voice quivering.

Masked outlaws were hastening to the windows, naked guns gripped in their hands.

The voice that Jenny Riddle last heard deriding her in this very room after she had dressed the wound in its owner's arm came calling thinly from the yard:

'Better come out of there, you Border Bunch *hombres!*'

The leader of the saddle-bandits, crouched under the largest of the windows, rasped a dry, mocking laugh, cocked the six-guns in his hands and shattered the glass of the window with the barrel of one of them.

THIRTEEN

The tinkle of breaking glass, caused by the outlaw leader shattering the window in preparation to opening fire warned the men who had newly-arrived in the yard of the Rafter R.

It was a warning that caused both Barradell and Merriam to yank their horses' heads towards the barns standing off to one side of the house. A split second after yelling to the outlaws in the house, the marshal and his companions were thundering in a flurry of dry dust for the shelter of the high barns.

The outlaw leader's shot was hasty and ineffective, finding its mark in the timbers of a barn as Barradell and his riders hazed for cover, hurling themselves from their saddles and seeking the shelter of the barns with their sixshooters gripped in their hands.

Barradell flattened himself close to the sun-blistered timbers of one of the barns within range of the house, Merriam close beside him. Their animals were hazing out of the yard, spooked by the sound of that single shot. Jed McAndrew and the remaining Rafter

R wranglers were bedding themselves down hastily, affording themselves of every inch of cover in the yard.

Another shot blasted from the ranch-house and a shard of dry timber was torn from the edge of the wooden wall above Jeff Barradell's head.

'So they want to fight,' Barradell growled. 'We'll give 'em fight – I only hope those girls are out of danger.'

'Yeah,' grunted Merriam, thumbing fresh loads into his Smith & Wesson. 'I don't want to see either of them hurt, 'specially Alicia.'

Barradell inched to the edge of the barn-wall, saw one of the heavy drapes at a window of the house stir and a black-masked face appear to take stock of the yard. The marshal fired quickly, heard the glass of the window shatter and saw the face disappear abruptly.

Instantly, a fusilade of fire answered from the ranch-house, the bullets whanging across the yard, some of them slamming into the barns behind which the marshal, the medico and the Rafter R men sheltered. It was desperate, ill-aimed firing and the men behind the barns were too well covered to take any ill-effect from it. Their answering fire was equally ineffective. The outlaws were sheltered behind heavily curtained windows and the men in the yard were firing blindly in the hope their slugs would find the outlaws. At the back of every mind was the thought that two girls were in the house and the last occurrence any man among them wanted was that either Alicia or Jenny should be injured.

For fully ten minutes, the pistols at the windows of

the ranch-house and those from the cover of the buildings in the yard cracked and flashed. Slugs zipped across the yard and the cordite smoke wreathed in sun-touched curls.

'This kind of tactic is useless,' growled Barradell to Merriam. 'We could keep on exchanging shots all day. I figure we should try to get nearer the house an' stand a chance of peggin' at those *hombres* at the windows. Fightin' this way is a waste of time an' lead!'

The gunfighting doctor ducked back against the wall of the barn as an angry slug whipped through the air an inch from his head. He unlooped slugs from his cartridge-belt and began to slide them into the chambers of his five-shot.

'Getting nearer is more easily talked about than done,' he observed. 'If we try to move from here we'll be cut down by fire from the house.'

Barradell waited until the slamming of McAndrew's men's six-shooters died in the background before answering.

'See the way that horse-trough is positioned almost plumb square in front of the ranch-house door?' he pointed out. Peeking around the corner of the barn, the gunslinging medico considered the stout wooden horse-trough centrally situated in the yard before the door of the house.

'That'd give a man good cover,' Barradell continued, 'if he could make it from here to there without bein' cut down, that is. Once he was behind the trough he'd stand a fair chance of pluggin' any *hombre* who showed his nose at the windows along the gallery of the house, an' my guess is plenty of those Border Bunchers would show their noses in an attempt to pick off a target so near the house.'

'And we could peg shots at them from here,' the medico mused. 'But you're not suggesting you risk running for the cover of that trough?'

'That's just what I aim to do,' the marshal replied grimly. 'The rest of you can cover me from here.' Deliberately, he began to thumb fresh cartridges into the chambers of his Colt.

George Merriam took a sidewise glance around the side of the barn and triggered a couple of shots over towards the stronghold of the saddle-bandits. He drew his head back around the corner as more answering shots whanged over from the house.

'You have a good fifty yards to run from here to the trough,' he grunted, 'moving obliquely across the front of the house – an open target for them!'

'There's just a chance I'll make it,' Barradell answered. 'Keep me covered an', if I succed in drawin' any of 'em into better view, give 'em all you've got. I'm goin'!'

He went like a bat out of hell, boots pounding across the rutted dust of the yard and legs working like pistons, running at a half-crouch with his gun clutched in his hand. Zig-zagging in his course, he ran pell-mell, moving obliquely across the front of the house. A crackle of fire sounded from that direction. He ducked his head lower, saw the bulk of the horse-trough bobbing towards him and hurled himself full-length for its shelter. Even as he launched his long body through the air, he felt the hot snatch of a bullet claw his leg. Then, he was behind the stout wooden structure of the trough, lying in the dust with cold perspiration streaming from his brow and into his eyes.

Guns were crashing and bullets whizzing across the yard in a hail of cross-fire. He edged gingerly around the side of the trough, saw a half-defined figure at a window fronting the gallery of the house and pegged a slug at it. A thin yowl of pain issued from the shattered window and the figure scooted back. More faces showed themselves and disappeared as quickly from the windows as the men over by the barns at Barradell's back cut loose with a withering hail of slugs.

The wound in his leg ached madly and he gathered his legs under him, trying to make himself as small as possible behind the trough. Whenever he saw a masked figure appear at a window, he came up from behind his cover briefly – long enough to blast a slug in its direction and the years on the owl-hoot trails had taught him to place his shots well.

How long he remained behind the trough, he did not know. All knowledge of time slithered into a blurred succession of ducking shots, coming up out of cover with a bucking, snarling gun and ramming fresh cartridges into spent chambers.

Dimly, Barradell became aware that the sound of the guns giving him support from the direction of the barns had grown in volume. There seemed to be more men back there now. He turned his head and, through the swimming haze of gunsmoke, had a vision of many faces appearing briefly from cover to slam shots at the now riddled front of the ranch-house with its bullet-shattered windows.

The truth dawned on him. The rest of the Rafter R crew, attracted by the sound of shooting, had come in off the range and added their weight to the fray which was, in fact the case. Whether their boss was in with the outlaw faction or not, the Border Bunch renegades were in the ranch-house and the whole Rafter R crew was making its fight against them.

Another figure appeared at one of the broken windows. Barradell came up from cover with a slamming gun. The figure stiffened then pitched forward through the window in a crash of glass to lie still, draped over the sill with a tattered section of curtain flapping about it like a shroud.

There was an air of finality about this. An odd silence descended on the yard of the Rafter R. Then, a voice called from within the house, a voice which Barradell remembered hearing rasping orders to the Border Bunch gunmen from behind a black mask during the battle on the Tucson trail. It came now, rasping, but cool and challenging:

'*Barradell! My men are all in – those who're still alive are in no shape to fight. You're a gunslick with a big reputation, we'll fight it out gun to gun, you an' me!*'

Jeff Barradell felt the pain of the bullet in his leg burning like a hot needle driving into the flesh as he heard the challenge called from inside the house.

This was the gunfighter challenge, a man calling for him to smoke it out; he'd answered to it many times before and he would answer to it now.

'All right,' he bellowed back in a voice which he hardly recognized as his own. 'All right, come out!'

A momentary silence fell over the Rafter R. The guns of the men behind the outbuildings were quiet. The flapping of the ripped curtain coiled about the corpse draped over the sill on the ranch-house gallery increased eerily as a gust of wind, strangely cold, came off the desert.

Then came the voice of the outlaw leader once more:

'*Barradell, a pardon for my men – they're all in! You an' me have it out an' yore men allow mine to ride for Mexico whatever happens! Is it a bargain?*'

'No,' yelled Barradell. 'Yore men are lawbreakers an' they face the law whatever happens between us! Now, come out an' make yore fight if you want to!'

A dry laugh came from inside the house.

'All right, damn you,' the Border Bunch leader called. 'I'm comin' out with my guns holstered. It's claw an' draw, Barradell!'

'Claw an' draw!' agreed the marshal.

Now, the silence was a physical thing, clothing the Rafter R headquarters with its heaviness. Instinctively, Jeff Barradell knew the black-garbed and masked leader of the broken Border Bunch would hold to his word. He would walk out of the ranch-house and Barradell would walk from behind the water-trough and each would try to beat the other to the draw. It was the pattern of the strange code of their kind – claw and draw!

The bullet in Barradell's leg stung hotly and he was aware of blood trickling down his leg and seeping into his boot. Around the ranch-yard, half-concealed by the outbuildings, anxious faces watched the door of the house and the man slowly coming up from behind the water-trough.

Another gust of chilly wind whipped across the yard, spurting feathers of dust.

The door of the house swung open and the dry voice rasped:

'I'm comin', Barradell. I have nothin' to lose!'

The tall, sombre clad figure came slowly forward through the door on to the gallery as Barradell came upright from behind the trough. His leg was strangely leaden, the nag of the bullet wound increasing as he walked forward a pace – then another.

The man on the gallery, his face still masked, came forward to the first step, a tall and lean figure, double gunbelts slanting over his hips and the curving handles of those glittering guns sprouting from low-riding holsters. As he moved forward, his hand went upwards to the mask under his wide-brimmed black sombrero. With a dramatic action, he whisked the black square away and allowed the stiff desert wind to snatch it from his fingers. His face was dark, hand-some in a brooding way and his wide mouth was drawn back into a white-toothed grin that was devoid of humour.

It was a face Jeff Barradell had never seen before,

but its revelation brought an instinctive moment of truth to him. In seeing that face, within the split second of the bandit leader tearing away the mask, he knew many things.

He knew why there was a heap of red sand on the floor of his living-quarters backing the jail; he knew who killed Bull Claffin and the Rafter R hand on this very ranch so shortly before and he knew why the gasps of the unseen men at his back came in loud gusts of surprise to mingle with the sough of the wilderness wind.

He knew the identity of the tall, gun-hung man on the gallery long before he caught a glimpse of Jenny Riddle's features, white and strained behind one of the shattered windows of the house and heard her voice calling, shrilly and urgently:

'*Look out for him, Barradell! Do you know who he is? He's Al Poindexter!*'

FOURTEEN

With the swiftness of a striking rattler, Poindexter moved into action. His two lean hands streaked for his holstered weapons.

Barradell staggered as a drive of pain shot up his leg from the wound, but he regained his balance and his hand plunged down in eye-defying speed. It came up from the holster, spitting a blaze of flame the very instant Poindexter's pair of shiny six-guns cleared leather.

In one moment, detached from all time, actions occurred as a series of pictures, each independent of the other. Poindexter's two Colts were snarling out their flames of muzzle-fire, but Poindexter was scooting back on his heels under the impact of Barradell's bullets and the outlaw's lead was screaming over Barradell's head for the marshal, his injured leg giving under him, was tumbling to the dust.

He hit the ground flat on his stomach, his gun flying from his hand as he went. His vision was blurred, but he had a distinct glimpse of the man on the gallery of the house going into a tangle-footed dance like a slack-jawed puppet, stiffening with a convulsive shuddering, then pitching limply down the steps to hit the dust of the yard.

Barradell spat dust from his mouth, gouged dust from his eyes, set his teeth against the raging pain of the wound in his leg and tried to drag himself up to his feet. He was aware of the sounds of jubilation at his back – wild cowboy yips that seemed strangely distant.

Then he saw, in one chilled instant which seemed an eternity, that Poindexter was not yet dead, that he was rising up slowly before him, that he clutched both guns still, while Barradell had lost his Colt.

Here, it seemed, was the end of his trail and the coldly grinning face of Poindexter, the man from the grave, the man who had become a symbol in his mind, would be the last human face on which he would ever lay eyes.

Al Poindexter grinned, the shiny six-guns came up.

There came the blasting belch of a high-powered rifle. Poindexter's grin froze, then became a twisted mask of anguish.

And he flopped over backwards to lie lifeless and twisted at Barradell's very feet.

Barradell staggered forward, clutching at his injured leg. Through a curtain of hazing gunsmoke, he saw Charlie Riddle, leaning across the sill of a shattered window, clutching a still smoking Winchester with his face set in remorseless lines.

Somebody grabbed Barradell to prevent his falling

and the dryly humorous voice of Dr George Merriam said: 'Let's go inside the house. We've had quite a party!'

The interior of the ranch-house was a shambles of broken glass and splintered woodwork. Dead outlaws sprawled on the floor. Only three of the Border Bunch remained alive, all were wounded and they were held under the vigilant eyes of a group of hard-faced Rafter R cowhands in one corner of the living-room.

Barradell was stretched on a couch while Jenny Riddle bandaged the wound in his leg from which Merriam had removed the slug.

Charlie Riddle, grey-faced and weary, sat on a chair close by, telling a story which fell from his lips with an eagerness speaking of his desire to be rid of it.

'I was a fool, Barradell,' he said. 'When I was a younger man, I was mixed up with an outlaw crowd. I got out of that phase with a whole neck and came to the southwest to settle down and turn respectable. I did well, got married and settled down here. I worked hard and built up the Rafter R. Pretty soon, this was the biggest outfit in the region and I was one of the most respected citizens of Santa Rita. I went on for years that way. When my wife died, I raised my two children and I thought all my wild days were over.

'Then they elected me chairman of the law and order group in town and I put several advertisements in Western papers for a man to take the position of marshal in Santa Rita. Al Poindexter showed up. He was one of the outlaw bunch I ran with as a young fellow and I thought he was dead. He showed up and held an evil influence over me – blackmailing me by threatening to tell the people hereabouts of my past if I didn't play his game. I pulled strings so that he was elected marshal. Outwardly, he'd given up gunfighting and turned to law-enforcement, but that was all a façade. He was slowly building up an outlaw bunch made up of picked gunmen.

'He located a hidden valley in the desert-ridges and that was where the Border Bunch had its hide-out. He planned to disappear once he had the lie of the land at his fingertips by acting as marshal. In that capacity, he naturally got to know about shipments of ore and movements of cattle. The Border Bunch grew and rampaged, robbing stages, bullion trains and rustling. Then Poindexter pulled off his disappearing act. The man who was shot dead was a wandering cowhand looking for a job. He was shot down by a Border Bunch crowd and dressed in Poindexter's clothing. The face was so badly shot up and the coyotes and buzzards had been at work by the time he was found that no one knew the difference.

'I played along with Poindexter because I was scared of him. Also, I was ambitious and fell for the line that Poindexter would give me more land once his outlaw outfit took control of the country around here.'

Barradell grunted as the girl attending to his wound yanked the bandage tight around it.

"You allowed them to run off some of yore cattle, so it wouldn't look suspicious everyone else losin' stock while you didn't, eh?' he queried.

'Yes,' admitted Riddle.

'An' you paid visits to the Border Bunch's hide-out, too. The red sand around that region sticks to a man's boots; it was on yore boots the first time I came here an' it was on the floor of my room in town – dropped from Poindexter's boots. How about that shootin' here – the day Claffin an' your man were shot?'

'It was Poindexter,' the rancher answered. 'I guess he saw you take Claffin prisoner from the look-out peak over the Border Bunch's hide-out – or his look-out reported it to him. Claffin was one of the cow-thieves the bunch used in its rustling and not notably brainy. I guess Poindexter followed you when you brought him here and killed him rather than have you question him and squeeze the whereabouts of the bunch's hiding-hole and the identity of its leader from him.

'He appeared at the bunkhouse window when Ed and I were in there with Claffin. I was so startled by his sudden appearance – I knew him from his clothing – that I called his name and he shot Ed because he heard me identify him. I guess I've been a good deal of a fool, Barradell. I only played in with the Border Bunch because I didn't want my daughters damaged by the truth about my wild past.'

Jeff Barradell gave him a hard grin and slapped a strangely comforting hand down on the penitent rancher's knee.

'I guess many a man has somethin' to live down,' he answered. 'I guess it's darned hard to change yore spots an' harder still to keep 'em changed once you've succeeded. To keep on tryin' is the thing I guess.'

He fell silent, self-conscious in the role of moralist.
The slender girl finished bandaging his leg and he
remembered the day she performed the same service
when he had a flesh wound in his arm. She smiled up
at him, the character of that quick-tongued little fire-
eater of the earlier occasion completely gone from her.

'There,' she said. 'Now, I'll make coffee for all of us.'

Barradell stood up and started to limp towards the
kitchen, and the younger Riddle girl came after him.

'Where are you going?' she demanded.

'To help out with the coffee. Any time I can't stagger
towards the grub, I'm really bad!'

In the solitude of the kitchen, he found Merriam,
who had finished attending to the wounded, embrac-
ing Alicia Riddle. He recalled the gunfighting doctor's
words at the desert water-hole the previous night.

'By the great horned toad,' he joshed. 'Here's a man
bein' tamed down by a woman!'

'Take yourself out of here,' snorted Merriam.

Barradell, grinning and possessed of a strange
light-heartedness, of which Merriam had seen a
shadow when the marshal whimsically smoked Butch
Albertson out of his cabin, continued walking forward.
His injured leg buckled under him and Jenny Riddle
rushed forward to grab him and prevent his falling to
the floor.

'I'm all right,' he told her.

'No, you aren't;' said she firmly. 'You need to rest!'

Merriam hooted a laugh.

'Who's being tamed down by a woman, now?' he

inquired. 'Better watch out, Barradell, that's a girl who could tame you if she was given half a chance!'

The marshal of Santa Rita looked into the smiling face of Jenny with its tip-tilted nose and air of elfin mischief.

'By grab!' he declared. 'If she don't get a chance, it won't be for want of tryin' on my part!'

And he was deadly serious.